THE STRANGER
WHO WAS HIMSELF

THE STRANGER
WHO WAS HIMSELF

James W. Swanson

ReadersMagnet, LLC

The Stranger Who Was Himself
Copyright © 2021 by James W. Swanson

Published in the United States of America
ISBN Paperback: 978-1-954371-93-4
ISBN eBook: 978-1-954371-94-1

All rights reserved. No part of this publication may be reproduced, stored in a retrieval system or transmitted in any way by any means, electronic, mechanical, photocopy, recording or otherwise without the prior permission of the author except as provided by USA copyright law.

The opinions expressed by the author are not necessarily those of ReadersMagnet, LLC.

ReadersMagnet, LLC
10620 Treena Street, Suite 230 | San Diego, California, 92131 USA
1.619.354.2643 | www.readersmagnet.com

Book design copyright © 2021 by ReadersMagnet, LLC. All rights reserved.
Cover design by Kent Gabutin
Interior design by Rey Alba

CONTENTS

CHAPTER ONE 1

CHAPTER TWO 9

CHAPTER THREE 15

CHAPTER FOUR 23

CHAPTER FIVE 31

CHAPTER SIX 41

CHAPTER SEVEN 53

CHAPTER EIGHT 61

CHAPTER NINE 67

CHAPTER TEN 70

CHAPTER ELEVEN 74

CHAPTER TWELVE 80

CHAPTER THIRTEEN 92

CHAPTER FOURTEEN 97

CHAPTER FIFTEEN 100

CHAPTER SIXTEEN 104

CHAPTER SEVENTEEN 107

CHAPTER EIGHTEEN................................. 112

CHAPTER NINETEEN................................ 117

CHAPTER TWENTY................................. 122

CHAPTER TWENTY-ONE............................ 129

CHAPTER TWENTY-TWO........................... 138

CHAPTER TWENTY-THREE......................... 145

CHAPTER TWENTY-FOUR.......................... 149

CHAPTER TWENTY-FIVE........................... 153

CHAPTER TWENTY-SIX............................. 161

CHAPTER TWENTY-SEVEN......................... 170

CHAPTER TWENTY-EIGHT.......................... 176

CHAPTER TWENTY-NINE........................... 182

CHAPTER THIRTY.................................. 185

CHAPTER THIRTY-ONE............................ 189

CHAPTER THIRTY-TWO............................ 202

CHAPTER ONE

RODDY LOOKED OUT at the world from inside a dark place out of which arose the heat that caused him to stick pins in Julia's dolls and strike matches from the fireplace matchbox and watch them burn because he liked their flickering glow. It was not at all now like when he stared at the flames of the campfires his family sat around when they traveled to the north woods where he'd go fishing with his dad, just he and his dad, not father then, Dad, as if they were pals and his dad showed him how to bait the hook, how to cast and wait for the tug on the line before setting the hook, and how to feel the differences among the strikes of the northerns, the tap tap of the sunfish, the slow heavy pull then yank of the walleye or maybe a large mouth bass, if it were down deep, or sometimes a surface frog that the bass would hit with an explosive whack. Wow, that was fun. And his dad would tell stories of the big fish he caught with his father, his dad then in the boat with him, teaching him as he taught his son now, and how they cleaned the fish like surgeons, he and his dad, who taught him how to slide the knife along the backbone of the bass and run it down to the tail, then just inside the skin to release a slab of meat ready to fry over the campfire in an iron skillet with flour and cracker crumbs and watch the flames whip around its edges and hear the sizzle of the fish in hot oil and breathe in the aroma, the indescribable aroma of their catch enticing the family to eat, then watch the tongues of flame licking the last of the wood and glowing down to embers perfect for roasting marshmallows to smoosh on the graham crackers with a square of chocolate for a smore sandwich. It was not like that at all.

    The heat was all campfire then not inside him as it was now or even as it began to rise in him as he flopped himself out of the hammock when he and his mother met that man at the cabin and he finding the matches in the shed and building a campfire to watch rise as it ate more and more wood until his mother warned him from the cabin window that he would set the woods on fire and to let the fire die now as he watched the sticks and even logs tumble like a building into the rubble of ash. After that the disagreements between his mother and father were arguments as hot as the campfires that were no more just angry words in the morning before his father left and the evening when he arrived home except for those inexplicable times when she'd coo and the two would disappear up the stairs to strange sounds and then smiles when they came down that lasted at least until after dinner when something she said or he said turned their words to knives and sent them each to separate rooms while Julia and Roddy waited in wonder. It had been so long since a real campfire, now only the match burning to match the heat inside and Julia yelling at him to stop or she'd tell Mom when she came home at noon and then he disappeared out the back door, and she found Sally on the front porch finishing her cereal.

    But that wasn't always how it was now, not with his dad who sometimes on Saturdays took him to his store, Mattson's Ace Hardware, just a mile down Olson Street, a street named after an Olson who had been a community leader responsible for the several parks in the area, a leader with a vision as Roddy's father had been in establishing his business to provide for the family, a hardware store because of his interest in fixing things, making things work, even if it wasn't his marriage, though he had worked as hard as he could on that but couldn't tolerate her philandering, her e-mails to not-so-secret admirers, her voluptuous enticement meant not only for him, while he watched his son and daughter disintegrating before his eyes knowing full well that he had punished them instead of her because he thought to defend her as the adult to whom children must be obedient even if she was wrong and hated himself for it, not standing up to her but knowing if he did the row would grow worse maybe to the point of no return that he wanted to avoid at all costs because he still loved her. So he took his son with him to his haven, the place where he was master of his fate even during the plummeting economy.

    Never did he feel that he would be blown over in a storm. He was master and his son could be master if he learned how, maybe at the hardware store where he learned about paint and door latches and replacing window glass and nails and screws and glues, and wiring and light sockets and silicone putty, learned to work with customers to problem solve a toilet or a faucet leak. At fifteen, now sixteen, Roddy knew about things other boys didn't. He liked being there. He liked greeting the customers and taking them to the section of the store that answered their need. He liked being with his dad as if they were fishing and fumed when his mother told him to leave the house, not him, his dad, Dennis, but it might as well have been he since his dad was a connection to himself, although he loved his mother's arms around him and wanted so much for her to love him and his father and sometimes she did but not now and maybe never again even though she told him with tears in her eyes that it was his father she couldn't live with, not him, but he loved his father even when he felt the heat rise in him so maybe she was sending him away, too, so he wouldn't bother her as if she sent him to his room forever. More than ever Roddy was sorry he had hit her when he had demanded her attention and she told him to leave her alone because she had things on her mind so that he thought his behavior was responsible for her leaving, for her anger with his father, her disenchantment for unrequited love, except that he, his father, had done what he could to please her from his pocket book to the bedroom and he, Roddy, tried to behave but sometimes couldn't help it and intentionally peed on the living room carpet after they took Chewbaca away to the humane society, the puppy they bought for him as an act of love then took away because that love was conditional, the puppy's and his.

That's when he began lighting matches, fascinated with flame, feeling deep down the difference between the campfire warmth and the flame creeping toward his thumb and forefinger until he waved it out just as it began to burn his fingers. Something deep inside him flared when he sat between the two garages a block away, one of which belonged to the Bentleys whose son Derek, the bully that dragged his toadies with him to torment Roddy, pulled his shorts down in gym class, tripped him in the hallway, called him gooseshit, that Derek who caused him to be ushered to the principals office for fighting where he sat closed-mouthed watching the vice principal and his dad shake their heads in dismay discussing his future, which according to the counselor should be very promising because of Roddy's high IQ and thus his misbehavior could only be due to an emotional disability. Now here he was, Roddy, striking match after match to ignite the paper and sticks of wood that soon caught and soon charred the siding on both garages, then creeping away to the park swing on which he pumped and pumped higher and higher, then bailed out and lay in the freshly mowed grass and listened to the sirens of the fire trucks, two of them for sure, that whirred to silence in front of the Bentley garage from which smoke billowed across the neighborhood forming a cloud over his head. Then a BOOM sent a torch of flame into the air high enough for him to see three blocks away while he now back in his room sketched a bat mobile. No one would know who caused the fire. Maybe Julie would suspect him when she heard that the authorities determined arson, but she would say nothing. After all they had a bond never stated but always known. Still he knew what he did and had to live with it, maybe confess, but he wouldn't. He knew that. It served Derek right and his family, too, who he knew were just like him always defending their son, the son of one of the pillars of the community. He chuckled when he thought of the pillars of smoke. That's what people like the Bentley's were, pillars of smoke, smoke enough to defend their rich lives but no fire to build a community. Roddy showed them real fire. No, he wouldn't atone.

The episode was over. What weighed on him now was where would he be when his parents divorced? With his father and with her, too, she said, Roddy and Julia with her, with him and again with her with two places that were their own, walls with different posters as if they were different people who were supposed to be the same. He and she, Julia, clung together now more than ever to weather the storm for which no end was in sight. It was as if their rooms had been blown away and they were left to pick up the belongings to reside in another place, nothing permanent, since their parents' lives were in flux and the children were in charge of whatever debris was left.

Only friends could comfort him now, friends with whom he acted but said little, nothing about the impending divorce, nothing to indicate that he was about to explode. Only Marty mattered now, Marty who lived two blocks away, a friend from school, where he, too, spent hours in the principal's office where they met. Marty, a crafty student with devious schemes to upset the system that was all too easy for him to manipulate, not that he hated it but that it was so arrogant in its authority over young people, especially Latinos, who must obey in spite of the havoc it caused them. So many, he observed, wanted to break free, not like him, who was free already because he had never lived by the rules. To him Roddy was a fascination, a kid with dynamic momentum that could easily lead to heaven or hell. Marty really didn't care which because the difference didn't matter. What was heaven to one was hell to the other. What mattered was pushing the boundaries until the who-you-are clashed with who-you-will-become. It's not that Marty thought this all through, but that he took a liking to Roddy, suffering Roddy, who had stuff about him that Marty wanted to engage and so did Roddy, who saw in Marty an independent spirit that would lead him to himself without the debris, the brokenness, but the inner power to transcend the life he had been chained to and take chances, make a move, stand up, sit in, sail off into the future, where everything is new, filled with wonder and chaos, yes, chaos that could hold him back from the security of disfunction that had been the mainstay with which he was accustomed. Always, it appears, that the customary seems the safest, the known juxtaposed against the unknown for which there are no rules and thus the threat of chasms into which one could fall and never be rescued.

Marty engaged him, showed him possibilities, led him into dark caves and glacial mountain tops and girls with comely smiles like Angel, the icon of young femininity whom he adored from the first time he saw her, who lived next door to Marty, who recognized her charms but let her be, not because of Roddy, but because his notion was for Juanita whose eyes told him he would live forever. Such is the foolishness of youth.

    He was handsome, Marty, two inches shorter than Roddy more robust and athletic and smooth in movement as if in sync with the turning of the earth and confident, wanting to nudge the limits if not push through to unknown worlds beyond his control. In fact, his world had always been beyond his control. He was Guatemalan, American born here in the U.S from parents, Jose and Isabella Martinez, who had escaped from the outskirts of Guatemala City, through Mexico and across the US border and had no papers. His father was a well-respected handy man, who seemed to be able to do anything and was busy enough to make enough money to live in this modest neighborhood. His mother worked in child care. His older sister, Clarissa, now pregnant, was recently married to Pedro who worked at a service station. Roddy was well aware that Marty, really Jesus Martinez, had many struggles of his own, especially the abuse he got from white boys expressing their crude machismo probably incited by Marty's academic skills. To them, no doubt, a smart Hispanic was as uppity as a smart black boy. Still in Roddy's mind he had what he didn't, a stable home with two parents and enough to provide the basics of life. He didn't care for more than that which in Roddy's mind was a little strange since his parents strove for more and most often tried to right their wrongs to Roddy with gifts. At least that's the way Marty saw it. What attracted Roddy most to Marty was that Marty seemed to transcend the difficulties of his life, transcend his modest life style and dream not of things but of adventures that called to him, some of which he chose to answer. How much would he venture?

What would take him beyond his comfort zone? Roddy didn't know and wouldn't ask but was willing to go with him wherever he may lead.

CHAPTER TWO

AS HE LAY IN HIS BED troubling over the events of the past three weeks, he tried to erase the memory of his rash, impulsive act that left his mother with a black and blue eye that turned green, then yellow beneath the makeup she thickened over the area to avoid public scrutiny, the act that left her afraid of him as he heard her tell his father and how he was like his father in his rage that he knew so well even though his father had never hit him and when he heard it, how he was afraid, too, that he might hurt her if he lost control from a temper that came from he didn't know where. He wanted that memory to disappear like his mother's wound to return to the beautiful moist hazel eye that matched the other and maybe it would if he could behave, if she would only pay attention to him, hear him even when he had nothing to say, just listen to him in the room, to know that he was there and now his father was gone, had found a condo a couple of miles away past the hardware store.

How he wished he could tell her about the matches, the fire inside that led to arson, that inner burning that would not have flamed if he could talk to her, tell her about his loneliness, his insecurity, about how big bully Derek pounded on him because he hung around with a Spic, and why shouldn't he fight back, then the principal's office and his indeterminate future, if any at all or to him, his father, who had now taken a stand but left him in limbo and whose stand had only to do with his marriage, not him. No, he couldn't tell him about the fire even if he would understand and if he did understand it would be even worse for both of them. Now he had burned down two garages and charred the outside of the Adams house, not the Bentleys because the wind swept the flames north instead of south. He didn't even know the Adams. So now his life was "her house, his house, whose house is my house."

Roddy had a Shogun Trail Blazer 21 speed mountain bike that his parents bought for his birthday, not that he needed a mountain bike but it would come in handy now since it was down hill and up hill and down again past the hardware store to his dad's condo. He said, his dad's, though when Roddy was upset with him, when he made him angry because he took his mother's side and when he locked him out of the house until he, Roddy, calmed down and could listen, that sometimes would last an hour or until he got so cold, he cried he would behave and sulk his way through the open door past his father to the living room couch, arms folded, head down, tears still streaming down his cheeks. When that happened, he called him Dennis. It used to be CD, Carmen and Dennis, as if they were an album of romantic songs but they were more DC now, like static electricity whenever they were in the same room. He loved his father. Why couldn't he behave? Why couldn't she? Why couldn't he, Roddy? and Julia screaming when she didn't get her way or every time Roddy touched her even. He hated her then and stuck more pins in her dolls and even lit a match and threw it at her laughing while screaming inside that he shouldn't do it. Why? Why? Why couldn't they get along? He had his Duster's Ace green and orange cruiser long board, too, good for going to his father's condo but not for coming back.

It was Marty that took the lead, Marty who had plans for Roddy, but had to entice him into becoming what he could be. Marty, who knew about the fire inside but not the outward expression of it and had yet to realize that Roddy had taken a chance, that he was ready to break the chains of his parents and his sister, and even himself so enabling to the family disfunction. Marty knew that Roddy lived in inner turmoil, struggling to be a free man, free of his parents, free of the angst pervading his soul. He didn't know that Roddy wanted Marty to help him, maybe Angel, too, but not yet, no, not yet, not Angel who was too innocent and at home with herself to fit into his chaotic life. He was just a Phoenix rising from ashes and dependent on a self-reliance he had yet to acquire and no means to effect. Yes, Roddy wanted Marty to take the lead while neither of them realized that Roddy was too far ahead to follow. To Roddy, Marty was the most independent spirit he knew: intelligent, assertive, adventurous, skeptical Latino Marty.

    Marty had a bike and a skate board, too, but used ones his mom found for him at a thrift store where he often got what he needed if not what he wanted and so couldn't identify with a logo and couldn't compete with Roddy's vehicles, though not top grade, were certainly respectable. But it didn't matter since Marty had long ago given up measuring himself by others' standards since he in his own mind was banished from social expectation even if not from Roddy who had the things but not the wherewithal to live up to the rules even though he looked the part but found himself too often in the principal's office with Marty with whom he felt a bond of likeness, not of despair so much as alienation. So the two boys were boys in need and invention to create a milieu for themselves that excluded those that excluded them and in which they imagined adventures, not in public waterparks or gymnasiums or skate board arenas, not where the other boys went, but where they could take possession of a space and live according to their own time until the reality of parental demands pulled them home, then off again along the bike trails or a swim to a lake island struggling through water weeds that tried to pull them down but never did, off to the "old barn," as they called it, even though it wasn't a barn, rather an abandoned train depot that once housed merchandise that would be distributed by truck throughout the Midwest, a place they found a few feet from the bike trail paralleling the railroad track and offering shade from the hot July sun and a private hideaway where they could smoke Marty's mother's cigarettes that he stole a few at a time so she wouldn't notice. It was dark inside except for the shafts of light that fogged in through the weathered cracks and illuminated patches of mostly moldy earth and a fire ring the boys had built from the stones they had squeezed through the larger holes. They sat on broken cardboard boxes once intended for packing but long forgotten as had this section of railroad now redirected through the city leaving it part of its past and a holding place for the dreams of youth, youth who somehow were lost in their present world, alien to it, angry with it, ready to fight rather than give up, believing something had to change, not knowing how to change it but not giving in to it, not beaten by it, so here Roddy and Marty sat smoking, saying nothing, watching the glow of the fire built from sticks and cardboard and lit with Roddy's matches that he never was without, watching it burn even in the heat of a summer day, dark inside, fire burning, like dreams in fists of flame.

On one occasion Marty sensed it first. They were not alone. He nudged Roddy. "Listen," he whispered. Roddy listened. Both scanned the darkness, pupils shrinking through the light shafts, then opening into the corners of the dilapidated building. "Who's there?" Marty called out, not really a call as much as clearing of his throat. No answer as the figure rose to full height and strode toward them through the patches of light and stood a few feet from the boys who gazed up at him unable to move. They could make out a bearded man, medium size, slight build dressed in ragged denim trousers and logoed sweat shirt that read Project Homeless Connect as he moved into the firelight.

"I'm Darrell," he rasped as if he had just smoked a dozen cigarettes. "May I sit down?"

The boys said nothing as Darrell sat across from them and stared into the fire. "I thought I could stay here if you don't mind. I don't want to intrude."

Roddy spoke first. "No, that's okay." There seemed to be nothing else to say.

"I'm sorry. I didn't know it was occupied. I'll leave if you want me to."

"No, no," Marty muttered, now intrigued by this polite stranger who seemed to want to be in this broken place. "We just come here sometimes. That's all."

"Do you have anything to eat?" He inquired apologetically.

Roddy reached into his backpack beside him and withdrew a protein bar and handed it to him.

"Thank you." He bit into it with broken teeth nearly hidden behind his beard.

"Are you homeless?" Marty spit out and Roddy nudged him.

"I am now. I was released from the VA Hospital three months ago and had nowhere to go. "I told them I had relatives in the city I could stay with so they let me out, but they live in Mankato and I can't stay with them. I stayed with them once before but my tantrums frightened them and they sent me to the VA and now I'm out."

Neither boy spoke as they pondered the meaning of tantrums.

"I'll get a job, I guess, but I lost the last one because I fisted the caterpillar driver when I thought he was coming for me. They didn't press charges, just let me go. A couple of weeks ago I went downtown to the convention center to where they offer things to the homeless and got some clothes and a pair of shoes and this phone and this t-shirt. The phone is only good for emergency contacts and doesn't cost anything. I check in every day at a shelter to see if they've found me a job. So far nothing. I volunteer there in the kitchen. I have to go there now. Nice to meet you." He rose without another word and squeezed through the crack out into the world into which all three of them were trying to find a place.

CHAPTER THREE

MAYBE RODDY DIDN'T KNOW what it meant to arrive at the crossroad that took him north to his home where his mother continued to keep him, or south to his father's new condo that was another place to live, not that he wanted another room to call his own, not that he didn't, because he could explore who he wanted to be, separating his old home from his new place in his mind and in decor even though he couldn't be who he wanted to be in either place because his parents had their ways of limiting his choices, at least he thought they limited them even though his choices often reflected his moods and reactions to anything they did.

He could bike straight ahead to the West Park Shopping Center with its typical suburban chainstores: McDonalds, Starbucks, a Godfather's Pizza, a Wells Fargo Bank, a Schulers shoes, a Cub Supermarket. In the center of the smaller shops next to the Fantastic Sams Hair Salon was Mattson's Ace Hardware, his father's business and out of which he ran a bicycle repair shop where Roddy worked from time to time and learned to make repairs. Roddy's time there was the only time he enjoyed in his father's presence lately. The two of them said little to each other beyond the necessary comments regarding customers and repairs. And his dad didn't over supervise. At times Roddy watched as his dad examined his work to see if it was done correctly and if it matched the quality he expected and rarely said anything other than, "Fine, good job." Roddy wanted more, but didn't get it. On the other hand, he didn't like it when his father gushed over his successes because it didn't feel sincere, like he was revving him up for a criticism that was hovering above him like a dark cloud of what he really thought and left feeling that inward surge of anxiety that might suddenly burst into rage for any unexpected reason. No, he preferred the minimal, a bare essential of appreciation.

Next to Ace Hardware was Pete and Emma's bakery. He could stop in there as he often did for a sample of chocolate raisin or oatmeal banana bread and wait to see if Angela, their daughter, would appear. He got to know Pete and Emma after his dad brought him in for a cup of coffee and a sample of whatever fresh bread was filling the store with an enticing aroma. Since then he often stopped in, especially when he and his dad were at odds. He discovered Emma, in particular, sensed when he needed to be alone and when he needed to talk. He didn't talk much because at first he didn't believe they could understand what was happening to him and that they would take his dad's side and make matters worse and Angela would reject him as some kind of freak who couldn't control himself which was true and that scared him. He wanted them to think well of him because of her and he hoped they and especially she would find some good in him. He remembered his dad telling him that their son, Jason, now nineteen, was serving in the army in Afghanistan and they were proud of him fighting for our country but worried about him facing enemy fire. He imagined him a hero with medals and worshipped by all and he thought about what he, Roddy, could do to be noticed. He was no hero; he was nobody and sinking further into oblivion and hoped Emma could save him or Angela or Angel, two lovely girls aptly named. He believed they were special, his mother, too--too special for attending to him; goddesses they were, to be worshiped, goddesses that were only attentive to heroes like Jason. But he, Roddy, had struck his goddess mother in the face and left her bruised and crying, his mother whom he loved and hated for not loving him, for not helping him become someone he could recognize, a potential hero, and somewhat understood his father's rage at him because of the way he treated his mother, his goddess, too, who might have been named Angel or Angela but failed to be her incarnation. He thought about Darrell suffering in the depot or walking the streets and wondered what Jason would be like when he came home.

But it was too late to go to Pete and Emma's. They closed at three to prepare for early morning baking. So he turned south toward his new place that he was determined to make into one portion of himself, his schizoid self. The thought of it both amused and terrorized him because he didn't know who that self would be and what agony he would suffer to become him.

He wanted nothing on his bedroom walls, nothing to associate him with a band, an artist, a chick, a racer, nothing that anyone could use to categorize him. He was nobody but himself, and he had no idea who that was. His room was large enough for a pine dresser and a writing table, both stained a maple color, that his dad picked up at either a garage sale or a thrift store and his twin bed with the Superman spread tucked neatly under the mattress and around the pillows. He hated that cover. The light blue sheets weren't much better. He wanted green like grass. Let the blue be the sky. That's what he wanted for those stark, white walls, blue, sky blue, with a few wispy clouds and maybe a planet showing through to suggest other worlds to explore when this one became impossible. He knew living things were not alone in the universe, even though his life seemed so particular, so anchored in here and now, mostly because he had to be constantly on guard inside the parental world in which he was imprisoned. He wanted this room to be a haven that allowed him his freedom to be whatever he dreamed to be, his place away from the there with them and inside the here with him. Amazing, he thought, his hideout safe from intruders. He knew his dad wouldn't enter unless he smelled pot, but he knew enough not to invite that kind of trouble. The only color he wanted in his cave was from his palette of paints from which he could imagine his world.

A few days had passed since Roddy and Marty had visited the "old barn," although they had wanted to revisit Darrell, but would he be there? Roddy especially, who wondered what was happening to Jason away in The Mideast if he would be homeless, too, but of course not, since he could be at home with his parents, Pete and Emma, and help them in the bakery and be back in the world of peace and prosperity, not like Darrell, but maybe like Darrell, too, homeless in his mind, where many kinds of wars played out in anger and isolation. Those battlegrounds he suffered himself. Were they any different from Darrell's? But then, maybe the war would be over for Jason. Maybe he just needed a job to set him back on his feet.

He called Marty on his cell phone that his dad had given him to keep him safe as he peddled around town with Marty. He was only to use it for emergencies except to call one of the four numbers entered into its contact file: his mom, his dad, and Marty. That was it. Cell phones were meant for phone calls and often cut out if not in close range to a tower. Marty would meet him at the crossroads after lunch, about one o'clock.

As the boys squeezed through the crack into the darkness of the "old barn," they heard:

"Tommy, Tommy, don't die, please don't die. Ya gotta stop bleeding. Oh, my God, stop bleeding. Oh, my God, Tommy. Okay, okay, okay, please don't die."

Darrell rocked on his knees as he tended to nothing on the moist earth, nothing the boys could see, nothing that Darrell could touch or save, tears running, muffled sobs until he saw the boys and tried to understand, tried to recognize them, tried to come to himself, then dropped his head to the earth and rolled to his side, breathing, sighing, then, quiet with closed eyes.

The boys stood. They stood, not knowing what to do, how to react, how they could help, what to say, or if they should go to him or leave him alone and go out the way they had entered. So they stood, until Roddy kneeled down, gathered the few charred sticks from a previous fire and laid them over pieces of cardboard, then touched them with a match he took from the plastic bag he kept them in to keep them dry. In the light Darrell seemed to be at peace, not at rest, but no longer shaking, quiet.

"I'm okay," he muttered and lifted his head.

"Did you get a job?" Marty asked to say something.

"No, but I will."

"Do you have any friends? This was Roddy's voice.

"Just you."

Did he mean Roddy or both Roddy and Marty and what did he mean since they had only seen him once? What did friend mean? What was required of them?

"You were talking about Tommy," Roddy said, trying to find the reality in the fantasy.

"Tommy? Yes, Tommy and David and Billy, all gone. Sometimes I see them wherever I am. Sometimes I see the guns exploding around us and then the blood. I can't stop the bleeding." He wasn't crying now, just reporting, as if he were outside the scene.

And now Roddy and Marty were his friends. If they slipped through the crack of that broken building out into the sunlight and went home, would they still be friends, or would they leave him with nobody? But they couldn't stay.

They sat by the fire a while longer until Darrell rose and said he had work to do and disappeared through the crack. What work, what did he mean? Roddy and Marty sat outside of each other, alone, wondering.

When the boys entered daylight again they looked down the trail along the railroad track toward the city. They had been downtown with Roddy's dad, but never alone, the two of them. Maybe this was the time. Should they follow Darrell? Marty said, no. Roddy wanted to but didn't want to go alone. They decided to ride a little way along the trail, just a little way to see how it went and where they might end up, how they might approach the city safely. None of his schoolmates would consider going downtown without a parent.

They peddled along side a ball park that would be alive in a few hours on this Friday night and all weekend. But for now it glowed an empty green in the afternoon sun. Ahead they could see where the trail disappeared into the dark underpass beneath Interstate Highway 94 then climb back into the sunshine and turn right up a hill to what they assumed was the street descending into downtown. Two bedraggled men sat on the concrete incline beneath the underpass sharing a bottle of something. Summoning his courage, Roddy called out, "Hey, you guys know Darrell?"

"Who wants to know, Asshole?"

"We're his friends. We're looking for him."

One of the men obviously woozy with booze broke into a laugh, then the other.

"You can find him in that can of ashes? Look in that barrel" and he pointed to an oil barrel propped for refuse. "Hell, man there ain't no Darrell. There ain't nobody but us chickens." They crowed and clucked and laughed until the snot ran from their noses.

"Fuck 'em," Marty fumed. "A couple of drunks. Let's go home."

Roddy stood for a moment watching the men whose laughter had subsided and who gazed back at him through foggy eyes. "I want to find him," he said.

"Go fuck yourself," and he turned away, no laughter this time. He took another swallow and handed the bottle to the other man. "Got a dollar?"

"Yeah, if you tell me where I can find Darrell."

"There ain't no Darrell, not anymore."

"But we just saw him an hour ago."

"No you didn't. He's gone. Give me some money."

"You'll just drink it up."

"You goddamn right we will, won't we, Gabe. Then we'll climb into that ashcan with Darrell. Give me some money," he demanded. He rose and staggered toward Roddy.

"Come on." Marty grabbed Roddy by the shirt and pulled him toward the trail, but he broke loose and pulled his wallet from his pocket.

"Here." He handed the staggering man a five dollar bill, one of the three his dad had given him for working in the hardware store.

The scraggly man looked at it to see if it was real. "You're all right, you son of a bitch. I don't know no Darrell. What are you doing with that Mexican? Ain't ya got no shame? Fuckin' shitheads." The two men rose and stumbled toward town. Roddy and Marty rode home.

In his room in his father's house with its mostly bare walls Roddy wondered what the ragged man had said about Darrell, if he knew him and was protecting him from inquiry, what he meant by him being gone, that there wasn't any Darrell, that they had never met him, but they had met somebody who was a vet, who had lost at least three friends and told the two of them, Roddy and Marty, that they were his friends, so there was somebody out there if not Darrell, then who? And why did it matter? Why was he, Roddy, becoming obsessed with this suffering man? Maybe because he pitied him, pitied himself, pitied being pitiful. That's what he was, both he and Darrell whoever he was, pitiful and angry. Pitiful and angry and wanting to find Darrell and be two pitiful people. Ridiculous. What was pitiful was his self-pity.

He wasn't like Darrell. He had two homes and a job in his dad's store and a school to go to and dreams of Angel who made his insides soften and the darkness disappear. And Angela, Pete and Emma's Angela, who would not allow self-pity, and for which he had no time himself. What he discovered was that Darrell had awakened something in him, something that took him out of himself. He was angry now, not because of his mother's neglect or his father's temper, but at the world that would turn Darrell into a deluded refuse of war. He burned with rage, wanted to burn something down. He lay in silence, breathing hard trying to still his mind. He had to find Darrell.

CHAPTER FOUR

FOR THE NEXT SEVERAL days, Roddy worked in the hardware store, saving his money, fifteen dollars a week, not much, but the work was fine. He liked helping people who needed mixed paint or some strong adhesive to bond the spokes of a walnut table chair. That's where he felt most comfortable with his dad, who was his dad then, but also his boss who didn't boss him but showed him how to do things, how to fix things, and what each of the tools and supplies was for. He liked that more than reading books like *Silas Marner* for freshman English class at Hopkins High School where he didn't fit in, neither he nor Marty, who was smarter than he, he knew that, and applied himself to get good grades because he intended to go to college and be an engineer or lawyer, careers Roddy thought sounded interesting but he couldn't focus enough to do the work. Rather he liked to sketch and paint fantasy creatures, robots, beings he might dream of creating in a test tube or engineer, yes, engineer with a pencil or paintbrush. That was another perspective of Marty that fascinated him, his self-control. He wanted to be like that if he could transcend his anger that often plunged him into darkness where he might lose the control he wanted so much to possess. But for now he had to find Darrell, to understand him, to see if he could conquer the trauma of war. Now that school was in its third week in September, he had fewer hours to ride, fewer hours with Marty, who seemed to have forgotten about Darrell as if the Old Barn events were things of the ancient past and hadn't enough significance to reside in his memory.

So now it was back and forth, back and forth from one place to the other until he didn't know who he was, his mother's son or his father's, not himself, no not yet because he was now three different people who didn't know each other and often was confused as to which son he was, and sometimes neither. That seemed the easiest, not to be either but the someone else who he had yet to find, the in-between one, the outside one in neither place, somewhere home away from home. He thought about Darrell who was homeless, making the best of being himself in a disturbed mind fraught with nightmares, not of his own doing but cast upon him like shrapnel so that he was never free no matter where he was, truly homeless. He wondered where Darrel's parents were, if he had any, if something had happened to them or if he had left and joined the army to escape from who he was with them, a prisoner, perhaps of their disfunction, or whatever, and he, too, Roddy, was homeless because neither of his homes was his. His birth home, he might say was only partially his, only on certain days or weekends and according to arrangements over which he had no control and the other a *tabula rasa* that he had yet to create but had no words to write, not yet.

Yet every time he suggested to Marty that they try to find Darrell, Marty had some excuse like it would be looking for an agate in a cornfield or swimming in a dry lake, whatever that meant. In other words, Marty was not going to go with him, Marty on whom he counted to lead. He'd have to go alone to the Old Barn or maybe the city, passed the ragged men under Interstate 94 overpass and the refuse barrels, where they said he would find their friend who didn't exist, though Roddy knew he did. He'd find him without Marty and soon, because the days were shorter and cooler. He felt more self-confident now having grown a couple of inches over the summer and filled out to look more manly, even robust, a physique of some power from lifting weights on his father's membership to Lifetime Fitness and with legs like pistons from pumping bike peddles.

Friday morning the last weekend in September, he skipped school and strapped on his Cabella's backpack containing power bars, bottles of water, a Leatherman all-purpose knife, beef jerky and undershorts, swung onto his Trail Blazer and started off. His dad, no doubt, thought he was at his mother's and she thought he was with his dad. Most of the time each parent thought they knew where he was, but didn't and hadn't known for weeks, and were surprised to get an occasional notice from his school that he had been truant the past week. They would have to confront him about that, but each thought the other was taking care of the matter. When asked about his absences, he explained to each of them separately that he was ill, to which each seemed concerned that he hadn't told them, to which he inquired, "remember when I had that sore throat?" And neither did. So it wasn't difficult for him to ride off into the fall forest of scarlet maples and golden oaks and birches along the railroad track trail to the Old Barn where he hoped to find Darrell.

As he approached, he noticed the soil torn up between the railroad track and the building and boards nailed across the opening that he and Marty had squeezed through to access the dark interior. A sign that read KEEP OUT and THIS BUILDING CONDEMNED served as a warning to him and vagabonds that sheltered there, which didn't prevent him from searching other accesses on all sides of the building, pounding on weathered boards, pushing here and there for a rotten collapse, but nothing, and no Darrell or evidence of him. Now he had no choice but to venture further into the unknown if he were to go in search. But why must he? What compelled him to find this man? He didn't know, except that he must try. It had something to do with his future. He had never felt more alone as if he were swimming in a vast sea among creatures beneath him or more appropriately pushing through a forest of strangers who knew more about where he was going than he did. There beneath the overpass were the two ragged men, one of which was called Gabe.

"Well, I'll be damned if it isn't Asshole," the other smiled. "Still looking for nobody, Man? Where's the Spic? Did you wise up?"

"No, he's smarter than I am. I'm looking for the guy in the ashcan," Roddy sneered. "You guys seen him?"

"You mean the phantom, the guy you called Darrell." Gabe retorted.

"Yeah, that's him. You know him don't you."

"Yup, sure do, but you'll never find him without an escort."

"So how much?"

"How much you got?"

"A five. That's it."

"Let's go."

The ragged men climbed the embankment, turned and waited for Roddy to follow. But he stood there straddling his bike waiting for inspiration.

"Leave your bike. Let's go," Gabe shouted.

Leave his bike? Follow these two bums? What was he thinking? He found an ash tree surrounded by bushes to which to padlock his bike and climbed the slope, squeezed under the pavement overhead and down the other side to Hennepin Avenue that passed what the sign called St. Mary's Basilica, then passed a pond and pavilion to the Community Care Center,

The Stranger Who Was Himself

that he soon discovered was a shelter for the homeless. It was late afternoon by now and a line had formed to register for a bed that night. "You'll find him in there," Gabe nodded and turned away with whoever he was.

Roddy hesitated a moment, looked back at the line of men and women all in need of a place to stay on chilly nights, all disheveled and weatherbeaten, like planks of human wood rotting in the elements. He felt his heart leap then slide back into its well-clothed cage at the thought that one of these untidy, forsaken men may be him. One might even have his name.

He pushed his way among them toward the entrance where he was stopped by a friendly doorkeeper who was processing one applicant at a time, checking off names on a clipboard, refusing a few, patiently dissuading others with encouraging words toward future access and suggestions of other possibilities. A few he directed to a window where an elderly volunteer handed out blankets to the unaccepted. The doorkeeper took Roddy's arm to deny him passage, but he was persistent. "I have to see, Darrell, who's inside. It's very important."

"Oh, yes, Darrell. You'll find him in the kitchen, downstairs, but you can only stay until dark, then you must go. Is he a relative?"

"Yes, Roddy hesitated, then blurted out, "My stepbrother, I think. I can't it explain it now." He hadn't plan to say that. He hadn't even thought it, but now that it was said, it mattered. It made him anxious, more determined that ever to know this man.

Inside he stood under a high ceilinged room with tent-like cubicles just wide enough for a bed and a night stand, many cubicles, maybe fifty with three aisles dividing them, two rows for men and two for women and a ventilation system high over head. Straight ahead the windowed wall of the office, maybe three feet above the main floor, rose another eight feet to provide for the many volunteers and the paid employees who processed the paperwork and overlooked the cubicles to maintain control but not high enough to invade privacy. Roddy walked among them, the occupied ones with curtains pulled across, the others open waiting for an evening guest. To his surprise they had real beds with mattresses. The place smelled clean in spite of the unwashed occupants. He wondered if they had showers. "Downstairs are the showers and the dining area," a shriveled man with a strong bass voice announced as he passed reading his thoughts. At the end of one aisle a sign read MEN with an arrow to the right and WOMEN with an arrow to the left and another pointing to the left, DINING AND SHOWERS DOWNSTAIRS. He turned to the left to the stairway that led to the dining room where stood several removable fold up tables with eight chairs around each. Under the upstairs entryway a large, open-windowed kitchen buzzed with the preparation of the evening meal. He could see the stainless steel ovens, stoves, dishwashers and dryers and a large steel door that, no doubt, was the walk-in refrigerator. There hovering over a large kettle of mashed potatoes was Darrel whistling an unrecognizable tune as he stirred.

    Roddy watched amazed at the size of this place and the facilities humming with activity in a most orderly fashion. He watched the mysterious Darrell, a volunteer, mentally present, dressed in army fatigues and a hairnet. He watched a line form in front of the kitchen window and the volunteers behind decorating a plate for each guest with slices of hot beef, potatoes with brown gravy, green beans, and custard in a cup. Darrell, too busy to notice Roddy standing a few feet away admiring him, smiled at each as he plopped another gob of potatoes on a plate.

Roddy watched the line move slowly, quietly, to the window, each guest taking a plate of food, thanking the servers, then moving to a table. To his surprise he spotted Gabe and the mouthy one taking their turns, sober it seemed, and deserving of a hot meal. When they saw Roddy sitting at a table they joined him as if they were old friends. Roddy didn't object, curious about these two that spent their time under an interstate highway and in a now condemned old depot. Or did they? He had never seen them inside.

"So what do you want with Darrell? This is Gabe and I'm Shithead. Thanks for the fiver."

Roddy shrugged his shoulders, not knowing the answer to the question he had so often asked himself. "You said there was no Darrell, that he was in the ashcan. Now here you are. You know him. You took me to him. You're his friends."

"Not really. He's a loner, doesn't hang out with us, doesn't drink much, doesn't want us in the depot with him. He goes there to be alone. Sometimes we hear him screaming."

"Do you know him?" Gabe asked, politely now as if the bullshit was over and he mattered. Imagine that.

"No, not really. He called me his friend."

Then at his right shoulder stood Darrell with two plates of food, one for him and one for himself. He sat down beside Roddy, looked across at the two men, and began eating without a word. They ate in silence for a few minutes until Roddy spoke.

"I came to see you at the Old Barn, the depot, you know but it is all boarded up."

Darrell's face reddened. His body twitched as if he were about to leap out of his skin. "Goddamn them," he hissed. "That was my place, my place. They had no right. Damn them." He jumped up and disappeared into the corner restroom.

Roddy was about to follow but Shithead grabbed his arm. "Let him be." And Roddy sat back down.

"We're leaving," Gabe muttered. "Wait for him. Ok?"

"Ok." Roddy waited.

When Darrell appeared, he seemed himself again but still agitated. "I don't want to talk about it," he said. "It's just that no matter where we are, they push us out. Not here, not there, no place. They want us out. We're a nuisance, nobodies. For Christsake, I fought in their goddamn war and look at me, no place to go, hanging out with other shell-shocked veterans and tossed away crumbs of nobodies. Shit man." He was shaking, working hard to collect himself. "You go now," he said to Roddy. It almost dark. "You have to get home."

Darrell's anger generated his own. Roddy felt his guts knot up, felt Darrell's fire burning within him, pissed at his mom, his dad, his two bedrooms, neither of which were his own because he couldn't feel they were his or who he was when he was in them.

"I'm staying here now. They let me stay when I volunteer. You go now."

Roddy went, knowing now where he could find Darrell, who he had to know and would find again and again until he understood, feeling Darrell's fire as his own, not fearing the dark streets, knowing only that he had a mission, that he had something he had to do for Darrell and for himself just a few yards from where he unlocked his Trail Blazer hidden in the dark bushes.

CHAPTER FIVE

IT WAS DARK, DARK ENOUGH so that an observer could only detect movement, as he searched out the ideal location that he found among the dry grasses on the north side of the building away from the tracks. He removed the paper he had collected from the refuse bins, mixed with the dry grass, stuffed it under the dry, weathered foundation, struck a match and watched as the fire climbed up the wall. He knew it would take. In minutes the building would be aglow.

As he rode west toward home he felt the fire inside subside. A calm settled over him. He had done this for Darrell, for the injustice of war, for the helplessness he felt in living his life, in trying to become himself, not knowing how to do that, knowing he had to make choices, and now he had made a choice for better or worse, for heaven or hell.

"Where have you been?" Dennis smoldered. It was Dennis now, not Dad, no, it was the angry man who couldn't control his son who was angry, too, because he always believed Roddy's mom instead of him so that it didn't matter what Roddy said, truth or lie, it produced the same result.

"I said where have you been?" Louder now and commanding. Roddy saw Julia eying the TV not turning to greet him so to hide herself away.

"I took a long bike ride and lost track of the time."

"It's 9:30 for Christ sake. Where did you go?" Dennis was trying to contain himself, no doubt thinking about a proper discipline but knowing nothing would matter.

"I rode out to Excelsior and met some friends. They bought me a hamburger and fries at the McDonalds out there. They're good guys."

"I don't believe you."

"Okay, let's say I rode into Minneapolis and hung out with the bums. What difference does it make what I tell you."

"You didn't go to school."

"That's obvious, isn't it."

"The counselor called and said you were absent two days this week. You were truant. That's against the law. A boy your age is supposed to go to school."

"So that's why I should go to school because it's a law. I'm glad we got that cleared up. I thought I was supposed to get an education. Shit man, I can go to school one day a week and get an education."

"Ya, you're smart, so smart that you're failing your classes. You must be learning a lot."

"That's because I don't do all that shitty paperwork, but I don't need to. I get it."

Dennis looked at him with sympathetic eyes. He had often felt the same about school, but had never admitted it. He seemed to melt as Roddy walked to his room.

"Wait."

Roddy paused.

"Give me a hug."

"Why? So you can smell my breath and my shirt to see if I've been smoking pot and drinking. Why can't you be honest and say you're mad as hell? Do you really care about me or is

The Stranger Who Was Himself

it more about you." He was feeling the fire rising. "Ya, I've been smoking dope and drinking vodka I stole from the liquor store. Can't you hear the sirens tracking me down? They should be here any minute. Then you can explain to the cops how your son is out of control and see what happens. What happens is that I'm going to Mom's."

Knapsack still on his back, he bolted out the door while his sister and Dennis watched helplessly.

"You handled that well, Dad," she muttered shaking her head.

Roddy biked north the three miles to his still boyhood home, the home where conflict was the mode of every day, but where he could escape to the room he had escaped to in every crisis, the cocoon really from which he hoped to emerge someday as a butterfly, no, a prancing steed, but horses don't break out of cocoons. No, his world was in ashes. He would have to be a phoenix. That's one thing he learned in school. Rising from the ashes, the ashes he made.

Dark house. Nobody home. He found the key under the doormat, a stupid place to hide a key, the first place any burglar would look. Didn't bother to turn on the light until he reached his room with his fantastical artworks peering down on him and across and he, caught in the matrix of his anxieties, he, wondering if his dad was waiting for the cops to arrive. He almost laughed then broke into tears. He really liked his dad. He liked his mom, too, even though she had more time for her boyfriend, or was it boyfriends, than for him. He thought she was beautiful. She must have loved his dad once and he her. And Darrell. God, he liked him. Why, he didn't know, but somehow Darrell mattered. He would find him again.

He removed his backpack and plopped down on the cream leather couch, punched the ON button on the remote and saw fire light up the screen. The 10 o'clock news on channel 11. He peered closer. It was the depot in flames and the commentator explaining that they believe it was arson. The fire chief in full regalia explained that while arson is a crime, the arsonist had done the city a favor after the city council had condemned the building and ordered it razed to prepare for a warehouse and storage units for city machinery. Luckily no one was inside. It had been a nuisance for years where vagabonds would hang out often building fires on the dirt floor for warmth, a real fire hazard. "It's fortunate that no one was injured in the last few years. It was a grave danger. But it's gone now." He smiled and added. "Let me just say to the arsonist if he's watching. Thanks."

Roddy flipped off the TV. He had done the city a favor. He had obtained his revenge and benefitted the city at the same time. Crazy. And the garages he burned? Both rebuilt, larger and updated, paid for by the insurance company, small peanuts for it, both homeowners were happy. His anger had resulted in a strange kind of grace, except for the insurance company. Strange and crazy. Somehow he felt watched over. The fires were over. Ashes, ashes we all rise up.

He was in bed now wiping his eyes on the sheets. No mom. Probably out with what's his name. Might not even come home tonight. That's okay. Alone and hungry, but not enough to search the refrigerator, more tired and alone than hungry, just go to sleep among the creatures on the wall.

The pounding on his door awakened him, morning light streaming in from his one window bedroom. The door flew open and his mother stood over him with her accusatory glare. "What are you doing here? You're supposed to be with your father."

The Stranger Who Was Himself

Arising out of his foggy sleep, he flopped back onto the pillow and muttered, "We had a fight."

"That asshole."

"Don't call him that. It wasn't his fault. I came in late and he was angry."

"So why did you leave?"

"Because he was angry."

"So it was because you thought he would hurt you. That asshole."

"No, no I didn't and don't call him that."

"Well, you can't stay here. It's not my weekend."

"Thanks, Mom."

"Don't get smart with me. You didn't go to school today, did you. The counselor called. What's wrong with you. I didn't raise a son who can't take the simple responsibility to go to school, for God's sake."

"I don't know, Mom. I don't know what's wrong with me and all of us. Can I have something to eat before I leave?"

Carmen melted a bit, trying to remember she was his mother, and wanting to be but not knowing how. "Hug me," she whimpered and opened her arms to him.

It wasn't like his dad's request, at least as he perceived it. It came from a deep need for both him and her, so he hugged her. "I love you," she sobbed.

"Me, too," he said into her hair.

"I'll make you some pancakes. Would you like that?"

He nodded. "Is what's his name here?"

"You mean Cliff."

"Ya, I guess."

"Yes, he's sleeping."

"Will you go back to your dad's?"

"I guess. Probably to the store."

"That will be good. He likes to have you there with him."

He nodded.

He ate the pancakes over-syruped, drank the orange juice, and in his room he stuffed his backpack, this time with a warm coat among his socks, underwear, shirts, pants and toothbrush. He took the sixty-five dollars in the envelope he had slid under the carpet in the corner of his room, the money he had saved from working for his dad and tucked it inside one of the zipper pockets of his backpack, half smiled a goodbye to his mother, unchained his bike from the tree and was on his way to somewhere.

When he arrived at the crossroads, he stopped on the side of the road. Straight ahead led to his father's place and his no account room, where he was supposed to be this weekend, from which he had escaped the night before from his father's anger and his own lies, lies that had become so easy to tell to him, lies that created a different persona from who he was, a persona he didn't like, except that he was better than the real Roddy, whoever that was.

To the left the bike path led into the city, passed the razed building he destroyed, passed his crime for which it was unlikely that he would ever be caught. Nobody cared. That was the problem, nobody cared, except Darrell, or was he making that up? Maybe he imagined Darrell was his friend, maybe it was all happenstance, that they happened to meet and he, Roddy, continued a relationship that Darrell would not have bothered to cultivate. Maybe, but he didn't believe so. Darrell needed him as much as he needed Darrell. That's what he wanted to believe and if it were true, he had to pursue him for both of their futures.

So here he was at the crossroads. His backpack weighed on him, his thoughts a burden, his memory of the night before, the room from which he came and the room to which he was assigned to return. No, he couldn't turn left, not yet. He had to see his father. Just being with him at the hardware store would be like an apology without having to say so, allowing his father to assign him tasks, greeting customers like a normal, responsible employee, feeling that possibility, recognizing his father's concern and apt supervision. He rode straight on to Mattson's Ace Hardware, parked his bike in back and walked in.

His dad half smiled a greeting, a smile of thankfulness but not a pardon. Roddy half smiled back, assured that he hadn't crossed a bridge already burned, knowing his father was still Dad, that there wasn't anything he could do to raze that bridge. That he cared. That was the problem. His own behavior warranted rejection, warranted grounding at least. Without it he could only feel shame. He hated that, but he came back anyway, knowing how he'd feel. Maybe there was some good in him.

Sunday morning. Nothing to do. His dad requested he go to church with him, but he declined politely saying he needed time to rest, to think, just be alone for awhile, that he was tired after yesterday's ride, even though his dad said it would be good for him to hear some "good news" and words of hope and encouragement and that he really wanted him to go with him until Roddy said, "No, Dad," emphatically, not wanting to raise his voice, not wanting to sound defiant even though that's how it sounded and that's how his father took it, shaking his head and walking out the door to the car and driving off. Damn, damn, damn, Roddy muttered, angry that he couldn't say it right, that he couldn't simply be left alone without getting into a verbal battle. Damn. How could he live with his dad or his mother when it always turned into a chaffing. But he had to try. His dad was right. He should have gone with him. What would it hurt? He could have done it for his father, given him a fatherly feeling trying to do what he felt was good and helpful. He could have done that, but he didn't and it irked him, just another example of his uncooperative behavior. But he would try. He would go to school tomorrow and all week, do his school work, follow instructions and the rules. He would do his best and then after school join his father at the hardware store, but stop first at the bakery to talk with Emma, and maybe Angela would be there, and he'd be a normal kid being nice to people especially people he liked. And today when his father returned from church with Julia, he would suggest that they go for a walk along the Mississippi River and maybe stop for a pizza and just have a real nice time together. Wouldn't that be great and yes, it would, so let's do it and so that's what they did and his dad, smiling all day long and Julia jabbering about the chorus she was in in school and how much fun it was and how good she could sing and they had to come to the fall concert in two weeks and they said they would and ordered a traditional crust pepperoni at Broadway Pizza because all three of them liked it, and Roddy was off to a great start as a normal kid who loved his family and even suggested they clean the house so that it would feel good to come home to all week long. And they played a game: *Sequence*, a board game with cards to fill five squares with buttons to make a sequence twice to win. Then popcorn and time for bed. It felt good. Julia was ecstatic, couldn't stop rambling on and his dad listened and grinned as if he was the Brady Bunch father of the ideal family.

 Roddy wasn't ready for bed and Julia, sensing something was up, plopped into the paisley overstuffed chair her dad had insisted on taking with him to his condo. Roddy felt close to his dad right now and felt it might be time to ask, though hesitant, then he jumped in like he used to do off the garage roof wearing his Spider-Man costume, except he felt this jump was riskier. He tried to make it a light conversation. "Dad, What happened between you and Mom?" Not a light subject.

His father didn't answer for what seemed to Roddy like an eternity. Roddy broke the silence, "It's about Cliff, isn't it."

Julia chimed in, "You mean Roger."

The name startled Dennis, "Roger?" He was focused now. "Roger?"

"You know him?" Roddy challenged.

"He was a high school classmate of ours. That's all."

"That's all?" Roddy pressed. Julia looked away red-faced realizing she had opened a Pandora's box.

"That's all. It would be nice to see him again. It's been years."

His words weren't convincing. Clearly their father was agitated and would say no more.

"It's been a lovely day. Let's get some sleep." Dennis left the room for his bedroom and left Roddy and Julia alone to ponder what just happened.

Neither spoke. Each searched the silence for an explanation that would somehow emerge like a genii out of a bottle. "Last night you were at Sally's overnight, right? When I asked if What's-His-Name is here, Mom said, 'You mean Cliff. It's the same guy who visited her at our cabin while I swung in the hammock and built a campfire. She introduced me to Cliff, an old friend. He left before dark. You were with Dad on a weekend trip to Wind River where he grew up."

"I don't know, but the man she introduced me to when I stopped by the bookstore one day was a guy named Roger.

Handsome guy, tall, strong looking with a big smile when she introduced me. They sat on a couch with a cup of coffee chatting and laughing like they were catching up on old times, so I left and walked home."

"Are there two?"

"I don't know, but Dad seemed upset."

"I know. I'm going to bed." Julia gave her brother a hug and disappeared into the hallway.

What had seemed to be a sunny family day had now clouded over. Roddy felt on the edge of a precipice as if some force was about to push him from behind, a force he had to resist to save his life and he would resist even though that force caused him to strike his mother and burn buildings, a secret force like a subterranean river gurgling in his bowels. And he had to see Darrell.

CHAPTER SIX

ON THE WALLS OF HIS ROOM Roddy had painted pine trees that coned upward from serrated trunks above bushy undergrowth so dense one could only see deep via the several paths that receded in perspective into darkness. He wired twinkling lights in constellations of stars over which he papered night blue with holes for the lights to shine through. No bed, just the carpeted green floor, over which lay a sleeping bag in camouflage fabric and olive blowup pillow. To him the room was a remove from the rest of the condo, a place away from the chaos of his life, the school he attended regularly now, his mother and her boyfriend, his sister who goaded him for attention. Well, that was all right, he supposed. She needed that even though his dad doted on her. Roddy had quit abusing her dolls or throwing lit matches at her. She even liked his room, liked it when he allowed her in, liked when they "camped out" together as he called it, she in her Alice in Wonderland sleeping bag, he in his. He told her that he met a homeless man, but wouldn't say where or when or who, just to say it as an introduction to the topic so that she would ask what it would be like to be homeless and why would anyone be and he said because they couldn't get a job, because they had no skills, or because of nightmares from fighting in Iraq or the long ago war in Viet Nam and he reminded her of Uncle Harry who they saw once in a nursing home who had a metal plate in his head and couldn't take care of himself and she shook her head and wondered about sleeping outside in the winter and he told her that some homeless leave for Florida, some sleep a few nights in homeless shelters around town run by churches or social services of some kind, he didn't know and she wondered how he knew about it and why he brought it up and he didn't know, just that it was something to talk about and they watched the stars twinkling overhead, here in their father's condo in Paradise Heights so named because homes and condos were built on four hills that overlooked valleys and implied edenic living, edenic, not his word, but what he thought outsiders assumed his neighborhood to be, not the escape it really was, not his escape inside the forest darkness that wrestled with his own.

He had a Macbook that sat on a small desk in the corner as if it had no place in his room, a computer on which he used to play Dungeons and Dragons, but not anymore. He used it now to draw, sketch inventions, people flying on the energy of thought, osmosis learning via electronic language seeped into a person while asleep, and modulations of the color spectrum in video swirls transforming in milliseconds in psychedelic patterns. And he emailed Marty, no longer talking about Darrell, just gabbing about Angel and how she was doing and if she ever mentions him.

He went to school on Monday as he promised and found it more interesting than usual. In social studies class the teacher took a straw vote on support for Obama, the results showing decided opposition. The dissenters argued that Obama was impeding the military from doing its job and failing to support our veterans. Roddy had to agree that so far Obama had had little success in including veterans in his budget. Though he lacked information, he believed that the Republicans were preventing funding for veterans hospitals and rehabilitation programs, at least that's what Marty had told him when they were discussing Darrell. That's all Roddy knew and was willing to support Obama on that one issue and the fact that he was a black man who faced a racist Republican Party. He didn't know they were racist, he simply surmised it because of all their attempts to discredit him, especially hanging on to the false accusation that he wasn't an American citizen. Those were the issues he argued in class to which the minority opposition aggressively disagreed, citing escalation of the war in Afghanistan and the increasing number of illegal aliens sneaking across our borders. The war build up disturbed Roddy to the point of a concession, but he still thought Obama was attempting to end the wars if he could get the Republicans to support him with international initiatives. And the illegal aliens business angered him because Marty and his family might be in jeopardy. They had never discussed it. He was sure that Darrell believed the Republicans were the problem, but it was just a guess.

That was the only school day in months that was worth Roddy's time, but a classroom discussion was just an exercise and no help to Darrell. Still he went to school everyday that week trying to apply himself. He hated math, but art class allowed him some leeway, let him create stuff, personal escape instruments, impervious costumes, and speed shoes. After school he stopped in at Pete and Emma's bakery and snacked on whatever was left over from the morning sale, often a pumpernickel rye or occasionally a cinnamon raisin bread with a glass of milk. On Wednesday Angela was there and sat with him for a few minutes, smiling as if she knew what he thought of her and loved it, but would only hint that she did. Roddy spoke up about the discussion in class about veterans and immigrants. He was curious about what she thought. She supported Republicans for their economic policy, but agreed with Roddy about Obama to end the Middle East fighting and liked his leadership. Okay, enough of that. He really didn't want to have a political discussion with her. Besides he didn't know what he was talking about. Had she heard from her brother in Afghanistan? How was he getting along? When was he coming home? Okay, she thought. He'd be home in three months, maybe. She missed him. "I hope he'll be all right," Roddy offered, to which she looked at him askance as if she had never thought otherwise. "I hope he'll be all right," he said again.

"Don't be so serious," she countered. "Of course, he'll be all right. He's tough. He can handle it."

"I know. You're right." He wished he hadn't mentioned Jason. He wished he didn't think so much, that he wouldn't get so angry at the world, about the way some people had to suffer in body and mind, about how many people didn't have enough to eat or a place to live. And he said so.

"You are a very thoughtful person," she smiled. I like that." Then she went into the baking room to help prepare for the morning.

He couldn't help thinking about Angela. He wanted to kiss her, but that seemed out of the question. After all, she was three years older than he. He must seem like a little boy to her, a confused, temperamental little boy. She knew he had problems in school and at home with his parents. He was not boyfriend material no matter how handsome he was. How does a little boy become a man to the woman he admires? Good question, one for which he had no answer.

But Darrell wasn't all right. He worried about him. He hadn't seen him in weeks. Where was he living, staying, sleeping? The nights were getting colder. He couldn't stay in the shelter forever. That wasn't allowed. He must be under the bridge with Gabe and Shithead and his nightmares. He had to see him. Why? He hardly knew him, but somehow he had become a best friend, an older friend. He was twenty-two, at least he thought he was, a war victim like all of those sent over to Iraq and Afghanistan, enlisted men to serve their country to come back with nightmares. He wanted to know what Darrell had seen, how different his nightmares were from his own, but did it matter? What mattered was how he lived them. He and Darrell, each in his private war, each living them alone even with friends.

Still he was only fifteen now, dependent upon father, mother, separated in two different houses each with a room for him that was only his for the moment and accommodated one of him, one his mother's boy, one his father's. Now he had committed himself to his father's requirements; then he floundered under his mother's absent presence doing whatever he did, just hanging out, pretending to go to school but wandering off toward the mall as soon as her car disappeared around the block, the mall that offered him nothing, especially the nothing of noisy, supposedly tough kids, who reeked of pot smoke, unadjusted teens flirting with sexual aggression, kids that he believed had no awareness of what really mattered in the world, or was he assuming too much? Were they all like him but bound now together in mutual dismay and resentment, expressing disdain for everything they had except what they needed? He didn't know but he felt nothing for them, certainly not their indignant expression upsetting the mall shoppers who demanded the authorities throw them out. How juvenile. How fruitless, how inane. So he succumbed to his mother, to school, to the shuffling back and forth, seeking and finding solitude whenever he could and the gentle smile of Angela, after school at the bakery and often at night in his dreams,

As the days and nights cooled to a frosty, then snowy winter prelude, he put away his bike that was useless on white, slippery trails, and all thoughts of seeing Darrell for months, hoping he was all right and Gabe and Shithead, too, still fearing that winter could take its toll. In the *Star Tribune*, he noticed that Hennepin Methodist Church was hosting a Ceremony of Remembrance for the homeless that had passed away during the past year. Suddenly, he saw the opportunity to pay Darrell a visit if he could convince his dad to take him to the service on that late Sunday afternoon in early December as darkness lay over the city. But how to approach it since he had never discussed the homeless or Darrell with his dad, yet remembering how his dad had criticized the government for not taking care of veterans to the point where Roddy had almost revealed his past escapades into the city, but didn't dare open the door to his multitude of lies. So he left the newspaper open to the variety section page where on Saturday the church ads appeared announcing their Sunday services and events, hoping his dad might see it. How surprised he was when his dad said that several members of his church were going to attend a special service for the homeless who had died that year and would he like to come to which he replied, "I'll think about it" then announced perhaps too quickly that he would go even though he didn't care much for church, but this might be different, so he'd go.

It was a simple service beginning with a welcome and an exhortation to keep the plight of the homeless and especially the war veterans up front on the agenda of all levels of government for better funding and facilities, the reading of a short bio of the lives of each of the 36 people who had died for lack of care and adequate housing. There was Julie Ambers, who died in childbirth under the Ford bridge, not alone, but without skilled help; John Peters, who was found floating in the icing Mississippi, an apparent victim of homicide from the bump on his head with a blunt instrument; several others who had died from untreated heart conditions, pneumonia and then: Darrell McClellan, a war veteran found frozen in the snow along the Greenway bike trail. Darrell, his friend Darrell. Was it he? He never knew his last name. Then as the congregation lifted the lighted candles in honor of each life, he saw in the flickering light Gabe's face partially turned toward him as if to assure him it was. Now what? Should he try to talk with Gabe after the service? Should he tell his dad all? Or should this be his continuing secret? As tears moistened his face, he saw his dad's puzzled face trying to discern his tears. Why would his son be so moved? His dad was touched by this show of sadness and hoped to inquire about it. His son had real feelings that he wanted to know about. Roddy decided not talk to Gabe. It didn't matter now. Darrell was gone, but not his memory.

"I saw your tears," his father said to him in the car on the way home. "Did you know one of those people?"

"I had something in my eye."

His father looked at him askance.

"I had something in my eye," he said again, unconvincingly to be sure, but how could he tell his father the truth, the truth that would make lies out of so many stories he told, the truth that could lead to the night of the burning of the Old Barn, the truth that would make his dad complicit in his crime unless he turned him in or live with the knowledge that his son was an arsonist and he the harborer of a criminal. No, he couldn't tell him the truth, but were there other truths he could tell or was he a condemned liar not by what he spoke but by what he didn't. If he feigned innocence of any wrongdoing would his whole life be a lie? And if you were a liar, was everyone else innocent or were all people liars, hiding their truths, putting on the innocent face for the world even those closest to them? Could he trust his father, his mother, certainly she had secrets from his father about other men. Did his father have other women, had he cheated on his taxes, had he hit and run. No, no, no, not his father, not his mother. He, only he, Roddy, was the liar, the criminal. All others were innocent. He could not bring his father to his level with the truth.

But he had to tell somebody. He had to find himself through atonement with those who could guide him to an honorable life, one in which Darrell and others like him could survive, one in which he could tell the truth to power and live with the consequences. That could not happen in his mother's house, nor his father's, but where and how? So he said nothing, living the lie as much to protect his father as himself so that they could live together even at a distance in the same house until he could find his way out.

All the while he was growing taller, not tall, about 5' 10", but he was aware of it as a force that was changing him into a presentation that had something to do with choice. His shoulders were broadening, his arms and legs were taking a manly shape without much effort on his part. Other than riding his bicycle he had taken no intentional exercise to increase his strength or his form except for an occasional trip to Lifetime Fitness. He wondered, too, if this was happening to his flesh, what might be happening to his brain or the mind that resides in it in some mysterious way like his soul or spirit which may be changing in spite of his attention. He was becoming a man in some ways, but he had no idea what that meant or what a man was, beyond a physical entity determined mostly by his sex organs. So what choice did he have in his becoming? Will the fact that he had struck his mother, stuck pins in his sister's dolls, burned down two garages, and an old railroad building, determine who he is, or could he choose to be a different presence in his changing body, maybe a loving son who will go into partnership with father in the hardware business, and maybe with his help expand into a corporation with franchises throughout the country? Would that be a choice or an unintentional evolution like growing another inch? Maybe choice means inserting one's will into what otherwise might be inevitable. To become must mean intention—will, choice. At the risk of another mistake, and he had made enough of them already, he had to choose and he would only know it was his choice if he violated what seemed pre-programmed. Still he wasn't certain about the contents of that program or whether his choice would deny it or confirm it, another risk of becoming. He knew he didn't want to be an arsonist or a hardware store owner, even though for the time being he enjoyed it, mostly for the people he served and the knowledge about how things work, and the proximity to Angela who was paying more attention to him when he sat for an afternoon slice of banana bread. As for him, his body was catching up to his interest without his having to choose. This was the good part of evolution.

Or would his choices leave him homeless? Was that why he took such interest in Darrell? Certainly, he wasn't interested in dying in the snow or drinking cheap whiskey under a I94 bridge. And he wasn't interested in serving his country that had no business in Iraq or Afghanistan, and failed to provide for homeless veterans. And he felt no patriotic duty to a nation that resisted every attempt to support the down trodden. He loved his dad, his mom, too, but the two of them were like rat poison in a chocolate cake and they were feeding it to him piece by piece.

    His choice for the foreseeable future was to do what was expected of him, go to school, graduate, help his dad in the hardware store and behave himself, or should he say, simply evolve for the time being, until he didn't know what or when. On his sixteenth birthday he thought his mother had outdone herself with the traditional angel food cake iced with chocolate and candles that she lit while playing the old Crest song, "Sixteen Candles," an insipid song that he hated to admit made him think of Angel again, "the loveliest girl I've ever seen." And to top it off his mom offered him a new iPhone attached to his father's account, of course, but still an expense for her and a thoughtful gesture supporting his first stage of adulthood, quite unexpected, not the cake or the candles, but certainly the mobile phone with all its implications. She hugged him and told him how proud she was of him, for what he wasn't sure and she didn't say, but whatever it was it warranted a new phone. He wondered if he did something to displease her, she might take it away like she did Chewbaka for piddling on the floor. He couldn't imagine a smart phone doing that. For now, however, he was grateful and thankful and hugged her in earnest. His dad's celebratory idea was to tie a ribbon around his Prius both lengthwise and sidewise with a big bow on top supporting calligraphic Happy Birthday. At first it didn't register as a gift, not until his dad said, "It's yours," did he understand. He floundered in misunderstanding. This was not something he deserved. Was it an attempt to change his behavior? A peace offering? Or was it a real gift of unconditional love. He could have traded it in on his new one, another Prius, but he didn't. As strange as it seemed his dad really loved him and believed in him. If it meant as a bribe for him to make better choices, so be it. It may work. He felt the need to do the right thing. Maybe he could learn to believe in himself. He was even ready to listen to his father about driving economically and servicing it on a regular basis. Now he had transportation and a job working for his father twenty hours a week, three hours after school, Monday through Friday and five hours from eight to one on Saturdays at fifteen dollars per hour amounting to $300 per week or $1200 per month or thereabouts accounting for the interference of particular events that shouldn't happen often. If he were to keep to his work schedule, he could easily cover the $370 per month insurance expense and gas, the stipulation with the gift. He acquired his driver's license after the second attempt since he didn't think he needed to read the driver's manual before the written test. The road test he passed easily because he had practiced in both his mother's old Camry and what was now his own 2004 Prius, in which he took the exam.

    Though Roddy enjoyed working the hardware store, he had never had a definite schedule. He hadn't fulfilled his school obligations, often running truant, sometimes days at a time. Now, however, he was responsible for his own car and, thus, regular work hours. He appreciated his father's generosity, but felt anxious about keeping to his work schedule, especially since he didn't trust himself nor his father to work together peacefully. So far so good, but they had never been sandwiched for so many hours without means of escape. He had always had relaxed hours that allowed him to leave when tensions arose or when he was inspired to do other things. Not now, but fine. This was good. He needed to learn responsibility and this was the most appropriate way it seemed to both father and son.

CHAPTER SEVEN

WITH A NEW COMMITMENT and modus operandi, he thought about his new freedom to go places as he pleased within the limit of his commitment, of course. He could go camping and fish. So he decided to call Marty whom he hadn't seen in months. He thought about Angel. By now she must be even more beautiful, like Angela who was often at the bakery when he arrived for a complimentary donut or cupcake with the purchase of mocha decafe. In fact Angela had made him forget all about Angel until that moment, whose memory stirred him and hastened his call to Marty. He surprised himself when the first words he uttered when Marty answered on his cell phone, "How's Angel?" To which Marty responded, "Bueno? Roddy? I hardly recognize your voice. Do you have a mouthful of birdseed? Donde has estaba?"

"Como? Hey, dumbshit. I've got wheels. Let's go."

"I haven't seen her for a while. She's going out with some nerd."

"You mean like you."

"No, not like me. Come on over."

"I'm on my way."

No more Darrell, no more homeless war veteran fascination, just a normal suburban guy with a Prius and not enough credits to graduate in a year. But that could change with a GED. He'd work on that. For now Marty and he would sleep in a tent and rough it, like the homeless except they could pack up and go home.

Marty was no taller but heavier, sort of bulky like someone who sits at a computer all day and eats tacos, but it didn't matter. They were still friends even though Marty was a science whiz and had applications into several colleges. Roddy told him about Darrell's death last November and Marty wondered why Roddy had been so fixated on him. "Because he needed us. Can't you see that? And the injustice of it? "

"Yeah, I know about injustice. You don't know about immigrants, do you. My parents have been trying to become U.S citizens for years, but so far remain undocumented. If any one made an issue of it, my parents could be sent back to Guatemala, but I could stay because I was born here and am a citizen. So they could separate me from my parents. Both Mom and Dad pay taxes and contribute to the economy. Depending upon the political wind, our lives could be fractured."

"Why can't they become citizens?"

"The laws are complicated. The reason my parents left was that my dad was imprisoned and tortured because of his association with drug lords, but he didn't know they were drug lords when he worked on a construction crew building their mansions. Well, maybe he assumed they were, but didn't refuse because of the money. The corrupt police considered him one of them and put him jail. But he was able to escape after a couple of months. That's another story. And sneak across the border with Mom. The problem is he couldn't prove he was abused, so the law doesn't allow him to get a green card. Obama has been trying to change that, but the issue of illegal immigrants remains unsettled."

"So how will you get accepted into a college?"

"I'm a United States citizen by birth. It doesn't matter if my parents are undocumented. They have to fill out forms verifying their income, special forms to report taxes without a social security number. They write in 000-00-0000. State schools will often accept that information and process applications for financial aid. Many private schools will too, based upon test scores and grade point average, of course."

"Wow, you know a lot about it. I didn't know."

"In my position, inherited from my parents, who are amazing, I have to know in order to survive, in order to make my way, in order to advance. So you see I didn't really get engaged with Darrell, not because I didn't feel for him, but that I have my own injustices to deal with."

"I get it."

"You have a good heart, Roddy. You're a good friend. Shit, man, we've even ended up in the principal's office a few times for fighting. You remember, what's his name, the big asshole that smashed my face into dog shit and you hit him so hard from behind with a biology book, he went down like a punctured balloon."

"And we ended up in the principal's office for fighting."

"And he lost four tires to a knife blade."

"You did that?"

Marty smiled. "Lets just say I saw it happen."

"So you didn't do it."

"Well, I saw my hand on the end of the knife that did it."

"So it was your hand that did it, not you."

"Right."

Maybe there was some truth in that kind of justification. The hand that commits the crime is somehow detached from the criminal. So is the criminal not who that person really is? Is retribution a justification for a crime that is somehow outside the person who commits it? But could he, Roddy, justify his crimes that way? No, they were still crimes even if the arsonist was not who he really was. He believed in justice, but floundered when trying to determine how to get it. Marty created his own justice. Roddy understood that, but was it just and would it do any good?

"Right now the laws allow me the opportunity to get an education. I may even have an advantage in getting into college as a person of color. But that can change. The conservatives are making an issue of illegal immigration and vowing to deport undocumented workers going way back. Who knows what can happen."

"Wow. I didn't think about that. But you have a chance. Darrell was permanently wounded, neglected, that's what got to me. You are endangered just because of your circumstances, just because you are trying to survive. I didn't know."

Until this moment their escapades had been mostly thoughtless adventures until they parted over Darrell. Roddy had misunderstood Marty's decision not to accompany him in seeking out Darrell. It wasn't for lack of understanding or compassion. It was his own circumstances that weighed on him. Roddy thought that maybe they had nothing in common except wasting time together. But it was more than that, much more. Now he saw Marty as a true friend who hung around with him because he understood him. In fact, he was waiting for this moment to reveal his real struggles. They needed each other through their private stresses, through the changes taking place in their lives. Now Roddy was on the maintenance road and he had the wheels to drive them around on it.

"Enough, what do you want to do?"

On Friday afternoon, the second weekend in June Roddy arrived to pick up Marty with his fishing and camping equipment. Roddy had the tent, the Coleman stove and the cookware. Marty needed only his fishing gear, sleeping bag and swimsuit for their weekend trip to the St. Croix Falls campground. Marty would share the gas expense. Roddy had permission from his father for the time off since he could make up the time any day of the week after summer school was over in two weeks that would grant him one more make up credit. He had three to go.

At the campfire that night only a few feet from the St Croix River, Marty strummed his guitar to the hum of mosquitoes, his dad's guitar, actually, that he had picked and strummed from time to time, mostly free form with a few chords of a popular Latin songs like "Eres Tu" and "Guantanamera". In between musical thoughts Roddy told Marty about the times fishing with his father, how he loved it, that companionship free of tension, free to simply gaze at the campfire for its beauty and its heat, its heat, yes, that served a dual purpose of which he was well aware. Of course, he didn't tell Marty about that, but did remark about its ability to destroy forests, houses, whatever stood in its way as the wind blew while Marty eyed him curiously as if to extract a secret. Then both sat quietly examining the fire. The next day early they'd fish along the the bank of the river for their morning breakfast, could be sunfish, crappies, maybe even a walleye, but certainly rock bass and sheep heads, not so good for eating.

They snuffed the fire as required and lay down to idyllic dreams. This was the life both young men could relate to together, beyond politics, education, or future plans. They had plenty of time to talk about those things but not now, not on this weekend adventure. This time together was for living in the now.

"It's good to be together again," Roddy murmured.

"Si"

They caught three bluegills and a crappie, just enough for breakfast after the skilled filleting Roddy had learned from his dad, a warm memory that produced a feeling of generosity. Things were going well. The angry burning had retreated to a warm campfire. And Boston baked beans from a can tasted so good, followed by a walk along the widening river to a popular swimming hole not yet occupied by bikini girls that would come later in the afternoon sun, one of the benefits of this campground.

Then the weekend came to an end and with it the resumption of duties. He continued the back and forth between mother and father, adjusting visitations based on his work schedule, but now with the freedom of his own transportation. His mom was calmer now, settling in with one boyfriend, Roger or Cliff? ready to sell the house that belonged mostly to her after the settlement. It wasn't a fair arrangement but a necessary one for a final separation, which, of course, wasn't final because, the divorced couple still had to negotiate the children's needs, rarely agreeing on what was necessary and who was at fault when things went awry. Both parents lived better lives with the least contact. The children that were now young adults vacilated between which parent with whom they felt most comfortable.

For Roddy, his Prius was his ticket to freedom. Of all the vehicles he might have liked, he was satisfied with the Prius. After all, it was economical and implied a driver who was environmentally conscious, an attribute he would gladly accept, rather than identify with a power devoted teen who doted on 4 x 4 pickups or red Mustangs or Corvettes. Not his style. He nearly vomited upon seeing a Humvee hogging the road, how brazenly destructive, how falsely macho, how insecure. Listen to the pot calling the kettle black. The mass of vehicles wasn't so noticeable on the road except in traffic jams but in the parking lots of supermarkets and especially Costco, cars, trucks, vans, atvs mostly with Minnesota plates but several from places like Florida, Missouri, Iowa, Colorado, Wyoming even California attested to the mobility of the American public, the freedom to relocate if only for the moment at one's will. People were on the move daily if just to the shopping mall but often on a road trip, a vacation spot, a summer getaway to renew and refresh because they could, because they had private transportation. Certainly, he was aware of the many Minneapolitans who took the city bus or the light rail for convenience and owned no automobile or if they did, used it for weekend sojourns with a friend or relative and also those who had replaced private transportation with an Uber or a Lyft service that was much cheaper than owning a vehicle, although limiting. People demanded the freedom to travel when and where they wanted and because of it much of the landscape was covered in concrete roadways and bridges which amazed him, thrilled him and repulsed him. Cars, cars, cars and now he had one and was glad of it, happy for the freedom to get away, to explore, to escape and well aware of the irony of his perspective. He was one of the travelers and for now to where really didn't matter.

Travel is not only a physical removal from one place to another, it is a transporting of the spirit as it was on this last camping trip with Marty which in some ways was a hiatus in his journey and in another way a kind of meditation preparing for his next adventure into the future. For the time being his fire had diminished to smoldering embers ready to burst into flame with provocation.

While the automobile symbolized an avenue to the future, the bicycle provided the contentment of the status quo. During beautiful summer days these young men continued their rides on the many Twin Cities trails, sometimes along the Greenway to West River Road and along Minnehaha Creek, around lakes Nokomis, Harriet, Cedar and West. Or starting from Mattson's Hardware, they rode west to Eden Prairie or to Excelsior along Lake Minnetonka and back through Hopkins to their starting point. These rides were therapy, a kind of meditation in which mind and body were perfectly tuned to red-winged blackbird trills, cardinal whistles, and the scent of newly mown grass. Neither lad suggested a ride into the city. For the time being Roddy was at peace.

From time to time he thought about Gabe and the homeless shelter, wondered where he was on those long summer days, who he hung out with, if Shithead was still hanging out with him, if he was drunk out of his mind. But somehow he wasn't drawn to Gabe as he was to Darrell. He remembered the veterans who struggled to live the civilian life after witnessing so much pain and death even if they were not injured themselves. Their injuries were to their spirits. He understood that. When he thought about it, it upset him. He felt the burning inside and saw the Old Barn burning, and lived with the secret of it.

His thoughts turned to Jason who should be returning from Afghanistan soon. What would he be like? When he stopped in late afternoon at the bakery, he always asked about him. Angela said he was fine and eager to get home in just a few more days. A few more days? Was that expected? Or had something happened. He didn't speculate with Angela, only smiled and expressed his wish to meet him because he had heard so much about him. Angela assured him they would be friends.

CHAPTER EIGHT

BUT RODDY'S REAL INTEREST was Angela. Jason was the conversation piece, the conversation jump start. He didn't know how else to converse with her. He was sure Angela liked him. Probably he wouldn't have to say anything, just look at her from time to time. He knew she was aware of his eyes on her and seemed okay with it, even encouraged it with a smile as she busied herself with clean up.

One Friday afternoon in the middle of June, he blurted out before he had time to think about it, "Do you want to bike with me after work tomorrow? I'm only working until two."

She turned to him with a look of curiosity and fascination that unnerved him. What had he done? Was he the biggest fool he could imagine or an impresario making his solo debut?

"Where do you want to ride?" She asked as if planning an outing with a girlfriend all the while considering what it would mean to date a boy younger than she and considering Charlie who had been wooing her every time she entered the Target store where he worked. Charlie, even though older, was handsome but immature, shy, maybe, certainly not impulsive in the way Roddy had just expressed himself. Roddy had a presence about him, an assertiveness that was attractive.

"Maybe Excelsior. There's a beach and a peanut bar there to hang out at and watch the sun go down."

"So we ride home in the dark?"

Whoops, he hadn't thought about that. Not too suave, not suave at all.

"Bad Idea."

"No, its a good idea. We don't have to stay until sundown. We can ride back and watch the sunset from Hopkins Park."

So, she really was interested, and in watching the sunset, too. He had never seen much point in that before, but now it seemed the most appropriate plan. It happens in the movies.

He didn't know how to think about her or about himself, his own body that evidently was attractive enough to entice her or was she just being neighborly or sympathetic to his difficult life if she really understood that and why would she? All she knew was the divorce and his problems in school, but in spite of those few details, certainly enough to reject him, she decided to go riding with him, she about 5' 3" tall and curvaceous and who obviously had the attention of many young men her age who hadn't pursued her, or maybe they had and she rejected them or frightened them away for lack of interest, but she accepted him, Roddy, for a bike ride and a park bench to watch the sunset. What was it with her and about him that enticed her or was he fantasizing into a disaster? He would have to play the part of a generous neighbor who wanted her to get out a little, to get some exercise, some quiet time in nature, always restorative for him and he hoped for her to. Would she keep her distance on the park bench or would she sit close? If she touched him with her warmth, he would stay within it until she moved away or until it was time to go after the orangy-reds through the clouds faded below the horizon. These images while he was trying to sleep. And then again it might rain. A movie? Did she think this was a date as he did?

The next afternoon Angela and he pedaled off toward the west, silently into the blaring sun. They had two lemonades on the deck overlooking the launches that were boarding for an evening tour on Lake Minnetonka, chatting about the various people in the party, not a wedding, perhaps a birthday for a 21 year old with friends and family. Sure it was, a young man's birthday with his parents and supposedly his first drink. The real party would happen later with his friends. He was the same height as Roddy with dark curly hair that flowed over his ears and down his neck. His body was firm and well formed like Roddy's, but his demeanor was more like the life of the party as he greeted aunts and uncles, no doubt, and helped his grandmother across the plank into the launch, a nice kid, apparently. Roddy observed Angela as they examined the partiers wondering what she was thinking as a 19 year old, as a young woman observing a charming young man. What were the thoughts that ran through her mind about him or especially about Roddy? Did she imagine what it would be like to kiss him and lie with him, their bodies touching, even making love. He had, even though, he couldn't quite imagine what it would be like except he was aroused thinking about it.

She said, "I think he's about to graduate from Carlton and head for the U of M law school."

He said, "I think as soon as this party breaks up he's going off to get drunk with his buddies."

"Really? He seems like a really nice guy."

"Nice guys do stupid things, too."

"So you admit that would be stupid."

"Well, sure, but he feels the need to celebrate, especially if he's about to graduate from college." He couldn't remember what college she said. Besides college didn't mean much to him. He couldn't imagine her choosing to sit close to him on a park bench. They were too far apart for that. So why was she with him across the table sucking on a lemonade? That she was gave him hope.

"I didn't want to think of him that way."

"You want him to be innocent when everyone is guilty."

"Guilty of what?"

"Does it matter?"

She was completely focused on him now, as if expecting him to reveal himself. Of what was he guilty? She waited, watching him, her eyes interrogating him or so it seemed. When he didn't continue, she let her eyes fall to her empty glass.

"My brother's coming home." The din of the launch party continued some distance away on the lake. "He's hurt." Her eyes stayed focused on the empty glass of lemonade. "You remember him?"

"Jason? Of course, but I've never met him. Is he hurt bad?"

"They didn't tell us."

Roddy realized now that she had been waiting to see if she could talk honestly with him, that this date wasn't as much about Roddy as about Jason. Relieved of expectations, he thought of Darrell and was formulating what to say, when Angela stood up.

"It's time to go if we're going to get to the park to see the sunset," as if it was a mistake to bring her brother into the conversation.

They rode east with the warm sun at their backs. Roddy felt the heat rising inside him. He envisioned the Old Barn burning and peddled faster as if to arrive at the scene of his crime in time to stop himself from starting the fire. But it was hopeless and he didn't want to stop it. He wanted to prevent Darrell from freezing to death. He wanted all the homeless to be in a warm shelter. He wanted veterans to come home whole. That's the fire he felt now.

All the park benches were occupied so they lay side by side on the cool grass slightly touching, looking up into the rose-streaked sky.

"I'm sure he'll be all right," Angela opined. He almost drowned once. Dad rescued him and pumped the water out of his lungs and he was fine. Another time he fell out of my uncles haymow into a pile of straw that contained a pitch fork the stuck through his leg. He was eight and he didn't even cry. He just scrunched up his face when Uncle pulled it out and rushed him to the hospital twelve miles away. He's the only one that didn't think it was a big deal."

Roddy wanted to tell her about Darrell but that would be cruel. He couldn't assuage her worry, because worry welled up in him. He prayed that Jason would be okay, whatever that meant. Hurt, she said, could mean bullet wound in the arm or maybe an amputated leg from a mine explosion or maybe no physical injury, but injury to the spirit, to well-being, to sound sleep and restorative dreams. Please not that. The body can heal faster than the mind if the mind ever really heals. Will his mind heal, his own? It seemed possible in the last few weeks during which he almost felt like a normal kid, but still a kid with a past trying to live in the present but with memories of his crimes. And what of Jason's crimes, justified by war against an enemy, shoot-to-kill policies that really weren't crimes by law even though they were for so many, of the heart. Could Jason justify killing because of orders? Could he, Roddy, justify his crimes that weren't really crimes because of the crimes done to him, or were neither crimes, just circumstances or consequences, the results of what had happened to him, cause and effect, no moral determination, just response, followed by the guilt, the nightmares, the self-loathing, the struggle in the quicksand that demands a saving hand. Was that Angela's hand, Jason's? God, he hoped Jason was okay.

CHAPTER NINE

IT WAS WEDNESDAY MORNING the third week of July when Roddy moped along the aisles of the hardware store checking the inventory to refill shelves of 3M tapes, disk and sheet sandpaper, silicone caulking and whatever vacancies he could see, not really noticing, not really concentrating, just musing. His dad noticed his inattentive demeanor, watched for awhile, then queried, "Something the matter, Roddy?"

"No, just thinking about Jason. He's coming home, you know."

"Yeah, Pete told me, said he was hurt, didn't think it was serious."

"I guess. I just can't help thinking about Darrell."

Whoops, he mentioned his name. He had never let his dad know about Darrell, even when he had the chance at the memorial service for the homeless he didn't mention him, afraid he would probe too much. Now the name hung out there in mid-air without support, just floating like a cottonwood seed drifting toward fertile soil that well might take root in answer to his dad's questions. On the one hand, Roddy wanted his dad to know about his adventures so he could talk with him about injustice and his unlikely friendship with the man who made the memorial service meaningful to him. When could he feel safe talking to his father, who had always defended his mother against him even when he was so angry with her that he exploded like a verbal cherry bomb. Yet he knew his father loved him, wanted the best for him and tried to let him be as long as he followed a few simple rules. After all he gave him the Prius. He trusted him to drive sensibly and to let him know where he was going and to take care of it. If his dad trusted him that much, maybe he should trust that he could understand what he had done and not turn him in. After all, it was over. No one was hurt. Insurance paid and the city was going to tear the depot down anyway. He had committed his sins in the dark and no one cared to bring them to light.

But he had to tell his dad something, something of the truth if not the whole truth, without creating another series of lies to facilitate it. But how?

"So who's Darrell? I've never heard you mention him before."

"I guess I haven't. He's a man I met when Marty and I were biking." So far so good.

"What made you bring him up now?"

"He's a homeless vet who had some mental problems after Afghanistan. Jason made me think of him." He hoped his dad would be satisfied with that explanation even though Darrell was still a cottonseed floating, no doubt, into another question.

Dennis knew he needed to tiptoe if he were to approach any closer to what appeared to be a door opening and checked up. But he didn't retreat. Instead he waited to see if Roddy would move toward him through the door now left ajar.

"I know I should have told you that we met Darrell and a couple of other homeless guys under the I94 bridge last summer and he told me about himself, that he was a war vet and had bad dreams and had no family and was homeless, homeless. That haunted me."

"So those were real tears at the Celebration of Remembrance last December."

"Yes. Sorry, I didn't tell the truth."
"Why didn't you?"
"I wasn't feeling I could. I wasn't feeling close to you."
"And now?"
"I'm not sure if I feel close to anyone."
"I'm sorry."

The matter of Darrell was over for the time being. His dad had accepted his explanation, which was the truth, at least in part. Maybe someday he would be able to tell him the whole truth. Maybe the justice system which affirms the innocence of all those not proven guilty has little to do with truth, only truth that fits into a small well-defined box. The whole truth lies outside the box.

The subject now was about Jason, son of a retired military man who was a defender of American interests in Desert Storm and proud to follow the competent lead of General Schwarzkopf. Now he was a bakery owner and operator, awaiting the arrival of his "hurt" son.

CHAPTER TEN

RODDY WONDERED IF HE should tell Julia about Darrell. Why should he? He hardly saw her from day to day now that she had taken up ballet downtown at the cultural center and he was either working or riding the trails with Marty. He missed her. He had long ago quit sticking pins in her dolls. She, too, had grown up, a young woman at fourteen who held the eyes of many a young man. He worried about her, even though he knew he had nothing to worry about. Unlike him, she had gained control of herself, having discovered that she didn't need tantrums to get her way, just a sweet smile and a tease. He guessed, and guessed right, that fathers were easily a soft touch for daughters when daughters figured it out, while fathers seemed to be the son's nemesis, an old story. Roddy realized that he was under his father's thumb just because he was his son and it would be that way until Roddy was his own man and no longer needed his father and could simply love him. Did he really know this? Or was he making it up as an explanation for the bind not bond he found himself in.

Yes, he should tell her as a way of bonding, a way of sharing with someone who lived in the midst of similar circumstances, who had been through the anger, the screaming, slamming doors, and he didn't know what else beyond his presence. Besides she had suspected some connection to the homeless when he seemed to know so much about them and had a real interest in such people. Again, however, he could not lie, but share limited truth. He could test himself in talking to a girl down deep or as deep as he dared to go.

He knocked on her bedroom door and waited. He couldn't remember the last time he had been in her room or how she had decorated it or even the last time they "camped out" together in his room, she in her Alice in Wonderland sleeping bag.

"Come in." She was lying on her bed reading a *People* Magazine, wasting time, apparently. Her room was pink except for the sky-blue dresser and dressing table with mirror and dozens of tubes and bottles containing beauty enhancements. Photos of Jennifer Anniston and Scarlet Johannsson, Beyoncé, Carrie Underwood, Blake Shelton, Alisha Keyes, and Adam Levine decorated the walls. Then undies, slacks, blouses, papers and rubber bands and a bottle of glue lay convulsed on the floor. Geez, what a hodgepodge. Could he relate to someone on her wave length? One enlarged photo of Julia in white ballet tutu on point in an arabesque left arm straight up and right arm extended out with fingers flayed as if to raise a cup of tea posed on the wall opposite her pillow. It was an 11 x 14 that their dad had given her after her appearance in the *Nutcracker.* Clearly she had traveled some distance since Roddy had last paid attention. Perhaps he could talk with her.

"Haven't seen *you* for a while," she blurted.

"And it follows that I haven't seen *you.*

"Well, duh."

Splendid opening.

"I've been fine," she smiled.

"I didn't ask."

"But you were going to."

"So how you been?"

"See."

"So now you can say, I told you so."
"What a mess."
"What?"
"Your room."
"I thought you meant my life."
"I thought you were on your toes."
"Clever. Only in ballet. You remember Sally?
"The friend you used to run to when things got hot at home."
"She's running with another group of girls, won't talk to me. I see Angel sometimes. You remember Angel."
"Oh, yes. Marty told me she has a boyfriend."
"I'd say several."
"Figures. I don't think about her much anymore."
"You were gaga over her."
"Yeah, I guess."
"So what's on your mind. Something's on your mind."
"I'm thinking a lot about Jason"
"Jason?"
"You know, Jason, Angela's brother who's in Afghanistan. He's coming home soon. He's hurt."
"I'm sorry. Do you know him?"
"Not really, but I'm worried about him because of Darrell."
Julia thought for a moment then recognized the circumstances of the name. "Was he the homeless vet you met?"
"Yes."
"There's more to the story, isn't there."
"He had nightmares, couldn't hold a job because he'd freak out with loud noises or cars coming at him in the opposite lane. Sometimes he'd scream in the middle of the day for no apparent reason and run, just run as if to elude an assault from behind,

then stop and cry over a dying friend. And he couldn't get the help he needed. He was homeless and now he's dead."

"He died?"

"Yes, froze to death last December."

"And you think Jason may be suffering such nightmares."

"I don't know. Maybe."

Julia rose to where he was still standing and threw her arms around him. They sat down on the bed side by side and said nothing for a time.

CHAPTER ELEVEN

THE ARMY AIR FORCE PLANE arrived at the Fort Snelling Military Base at noon and then the MPs transported Jason to Veterans Hospital where he continued treatment for several days. No longer critical, he still required extensive care and rehabilitation. Pete and Emma and Angela had yet to learn the extent of his injuries, but were assured he was on his way to recovery, whatever that meant. Dennis, Roddy, and Julia waited to hear. It was too soon for them to welcome him home. Since Mattson's Ace Hardware and Golden Bakery were side by side in the shopping center, Dennis and the Johnsons had become good friends. They had shared with him the play by play adventures of their son, to whatever extent he, Jason, was willing to share. As far as they knew Jason was feeling positive about his experience and the role he was playing in protecting the Afghanis and defeating the Talaban.

That was important to Pete, a long time supporter of American military initiatives in the Mideast and an avid ex-marine. Enlisted men, in his estimation, were our heroes fighting for democracy and our values. It was with pride and trepidation that he and his wife drove to the VA to see their son for the first time in almost a year. How severe were his injuries? Would he recover fully? It never occurred to him that his son may be psychologically damaged, not his son, not his courageous son, who was strong in both mind and body. Certainly, both could withstand an enemy assault. If he had escaped with his life, he would recover. He believed that.

Dennis wasn't so sure and Roddy fearful. Julia was mostly concerned about Roddy who she hoped would not have to face another shell-shocked vet with inadequate health care. At least Jason wouldn't be homeless. Neither she nor Jason had met him, but both prayed for his return to health. They felt they knew him through reports and stories. They had seen many photos of him with his Army buddies with AK 47's at their sides laughing as if they had just finished taking a Talaban stronghold or about to be on weekend leave to drink a few beers. Photos and stories were all they knew of him and were waiting to learn more wondering if they would recognize that smiling face and when.

In meantime Roddy was at play, Roddy and Marty, the twosome again. They could be Army buddies if either of them was interested in becoming a soldier. No way, Jose, for either. Neither agreed with Pete Johnson that our military deployments were smart or justified. Neither believed them to be worthy efforts for which one would endanger his life. Most of the recruits it appeared were those who thought the service provided them with a job better than what they could acquire in civilian life while the nation ignored them and their sacrifice.

Still Roddy was attracted to the adventure, even, he had to admit, the danger, the test of his courage, the chance to be a hero, to be part of a close knit group working together for a cause. It was that, perhaps, that had attracted him to Darrell, for whom he felt a commitment, a connection because of the injustice of his post-war plight, the lack of support except through charities like shelters and food shelfs. Even Darrell's pain over the loss of Tommy enticed him. Darrell had clearly bonded with his Army buddies. Marty was a friend, yes, but would Roddy die for him? Would he die for anything? What really mattered to him? To whom did he really matter? Maybe his mom and dad and Julia, who were often Dennis and Carmen at odds with his contentious behavior, especially his truancies. He didn't like school. It seemed confining and misdirected. He knew he needed the skills, some of which he wasn't getting, but he would somehow. But what he wanted most was adventure, a challenge of his own making. He was more eager to know Jason now as he recouped from injuries. He wanted to know if he was as strong as his dad, Peter, and believed he would be. He wanted to hear his stories. He wanted to know if he believed he had met the test. He even wondered if he wore a "red badge of courage," a real one, not one acquired under retreat. A book by that name was required reading in his English class and one of the few book he had read. Roddy waited and went camping with Marty.

    Summer school was a drag. He stayed with it. He had promised his parents and himself that he would, but he applied himself only enough to get the credit, except for writing. He liked writing his thoughts on paper even if they weren't in compliance with the assignment. His teacher wanted an organized three paragraph essay. Roddy wanted to vent, helter shelter vent. What he learned, however, was that even venting needed structure and that writing could be a focused attempt to communicate with a reader, not just a diarrhea of the mind. He discovered that this teacher, Mr. Sanchez, seemed to understand his need, even accepted his babbling as legitimate thoughts to be explored and helped him channel them in a way he hadn't done before. He wrote a persuasive essay, an actual essay on the societies lack of response to wounded soldiers and Sanchez read it to the class. His teacher affirmed his effort, legitimized his thinking, opened the topic for discussion. Never before had Roddy felt such affirmation. Never had he considered the written word as a tool. Now he had to figure out how to use it. So he finished summer school and got the credit. Still he lacked the credits to graduate on time. He would need a post-graduation summer school and he would have to pass all of his classes his senior year.

As they sat across from each other at the kitchen table, Roddy and his dad ate the fried eggs and wheat toast his dad had cooked for breakfast. Roddy, however, fidgeted until he broke the silence with his assertion. He didn't ask, he told his dad that he and Marty were going on adventure in the Boundary Waters and was taking time off from work but would make it up and not neglect his financial obligations. In fact, in addition to paying for his car insurance and keeping it in gas, he was saving money. He had already put away $300 in the account his father helped him set up at Wells Fargo. Of that he was quite proud.

"Sounds like a plan, but a bit flawed. Let me tell you," his dad began. He always started a lecture with that phrase even though he didn't intend to lecture. "You'll have to rent a canoe, let's say $50 a day and a Duluth pack for transporting your cook ware, food, ax, rope, matches, flashlight, tackle box, Swiss Army knife, etc, another $50 per day." How long are you going to be gone? Hmmm. How about the permit for which you need to apply well in advance, since the Boundary Waters are restricted to permitted persons only and all persons under 18 years of age have to be accompanied by an adult and I'm not available. Besides it's already July and all permits are, no doubt, distributed through the summer. Nope, no Boundary Waters this year. Maybe next year."

Roddy stared at his dad, Dennis now. "You know you always have to bring me down," he snarled, feeling the heat rising. He felt his father's thumb pressing on him like a heavy stone that wouldn't let him breathe.

"I don't mean to bring you down, as you say, but you have to face the facts. Go camping, but not to the Boundary Waters. Go south, southeastern Minnesota is a beautiful area with rivers and rolling hills. Check it out. You don't need a canoe or a lot of equipment and you're never far away from a convenience store if you need something."

Roddy felt himself cooling but wasn't ready to engage in conversation. Rather, he got up, took his plate, knife and fork to the sink and walked, didn't march, or saunter, just walked through the door to his room and slammed it. The slam would be enough to clarify his response. All right, no Boundary Waters. He had to admit his dad was right, but he wasn't going to. He lay on his bed fuming, a soft fume, but still a fume, then took his seat at his desk and opened his laptop. Camping in southeastern Minnesota. He saw several— Lake City, Wabasha, Whitewater, Zumbrota, Cannon Falls, and rivers coming from north and south to flow into the Mississippi River. He felt the weight of Dennis' thumb lift. His dad knew what he was talking about. This could be good. All he and Marty would need were the basics. They could drive until they found an isolated place and explore. Roddy had a bike rack that would fit on his Prius and they both had back packs that would hold enough. Back in the kitchen his dad was reading the *Star Tribune*, still at the breakfast table. He looked up. "Well, what did you decide?".

"I don't know." Even though he knew his dad was right, he didn't want to admit it. "I'll talk it over with Marty. Can I take next week off?"

"Not a problem. But I have to know where you're going, so does your Mom. I'll miss you, you know."

That was good to hear. He felt better. "See ya later, Dad."

His father smiled, but tried hard not to make it an I-told-you-so smile.

The two boys studied the road map, looked up the topography of the area and decided on a route following the Mississippi River and then west into the rolling hills cut through with rivers and valleys. Somewhere they would find the place where they could fish for trout with spinners and worms that they could dig up or, if need be, buy at a Casey's or Holiday service station. They'd find fire wood, or buy that, too. Marty didn't need time off because he didn't have a job. He was studying philosophy and mathematics. He loved Descartes, but told Roddy he was struggling with Kant, to which Roddy shrugged, "Cant get Kant, huh?" He made them rhyme. That's as close as Roddy would get to studying the philosophers, though he enjoyed talking with Marty about them. He liked the idea that the idea of things was real and the image through which the thing was made. Plato, he remembered, said something like that. He was also aware that our senses deceive us, a mirage is a good example or the direction of a sound. He was struck by the reality question. Marty called it "metaphysical." A trip with Marty would be fine. Let the two of them learn from each other. Roddy knew how to use tools and could figure out how to fix just about anything and a thousand uses for duct tape, rope, Gorilla glue, and WD40. Those items went in their back packs for sure. What else? He'd think about it. He thought about Darrell and what he could have learned from him and then Jason. He needed to talk with Jason. He had questions for him.

CHAPTER TWELVE

ON A BEAUTIFUL SUNDAY morning in late July, Roddy declined to go to church with his mother, told her he was going with Marty camping in Southeastern Minnesota, somewhere among the deciduous forests and rivers, then sped his Prius out of the parking lot to pick up Marty. The Prius trunk was packed. The bike rack fit perfectly. The sun was shining and Marty was ready. The two boys could be driving off to Neverland, and maybe they were, at least to a land that was a different reality, a boy's reality, driving into their future, whatever it might be.

It was dry, so dry. It hadn't rained for days. Maybe the rivers would be only trickles with stagnant water and mosquitoes. Maybe the leaves would crackle in the breeze like cellophane wrap or Doritos. Maybe, but who cared. They would create their adventure in the peopleless woods.

They started down highway 62 to 55 and south toward Hastings, took the cutoff on 319 to catch up to 61 again, then into Redwing, down through Lake City to Wabash and inland on 60 toward Zumbrota. Just driving, no radio, no conversation, just driving and gazing at the lush banks of oaks, maples, and birches and the ever so gently churning Mississippi River that first peeked in across the railroad tracks through the trees, then opened from the vast expanse of Lake Pepin. How beautiful and easy, it seemed. What would it be like to live in these parts, so sparsely populated in small towns clinging to the river, owning touristy kinds of business or a cafe or a grocery store, instead of living in the suburbs or the city with its homeless. The thought came back to him. It never absented itself for long. Were there homeless in the country? Were people living off the land. Did they have enough to eat?

Up they climbed away from the river past a golf course, then winding down into valleys and up onto the plains of corn and soybeans. Nice farm houses isolated among the fields with sturdy outbuildings housing tractors and corn pickers and certainly riding lawn mowers to clip the vast yards rolling around these properties. In one valley a river wound through a small town and passed under a bridge along the Main Street where Bertha's Family Diner parked behind a sidewalk, and beside it a post office, a grocery store and a service station. A sign high on a telephone pole read, "Flood level 2010." Clearly only the tops of these shops could poke above such a flood stage, but they had been restored. The town remained. Business as usual.

They stopped at Bertha's for a broasted chicken with canned green beans, mashed potatoes, and a custard dessert. Nothing special but good enough with the added entertainment of an elderly man whose wife sat quietly across from him at the next table, a man who was convinced that Roddy looked exactly like his brother's kid in Ohio.

"Excuse me, son, but I have to tell you, you look exactly like my brother's kid in Ohio. In fact, I would swear you were my brother's kid if I didn't know that my brother and family were nowhere near here. They're in Ohio, but you sure look like my nephew Corey. What's your name?" He nodded to Roddy.

"Roddy," Roddy smiled. "I guess I have a familiar face."

"No, I don't think so, because I've never seen any face that looked so much like Corey's. You're smaller and not as heavy as Corey, but your face is a splitting image. Tell me, son, are you going to college?"

"No, I'm still in high school. I'll be a senior in the fall."

"My nephew Corey is going to Ohio State. He plays football, a line backer and a good one. He can stand a running back straight up at the line like no one I've ever seen. Wants to be a pro, and he'll make it. I can't get over how much you look like him. What did you say your name is?"

"Roddy. Are there any campgrounds around here?" He nearly shouted to the waitress, an attractive middle-aged woman who realized she was called to the rescue.

The elderly man started an answer, but the waitress cut him off with "I'll explain it, Fred."

"It isn't hard to find the County one," he continued.

"No it isn't. It's a nice one right down the road," she continued.

Which way you going?"

Roddy pointed West.

"Yeah, you just keep right on 60 then when you come to the road just beyond the huge metal pole barn on the left side of the road, turn left. There's a sign there that says, "County campground, but it's hard to see. Follow that road a mile or so. It'll twist and turn a bit but it's a nice campground along the river."

"Thanks for your help," Marty smiled and walked to the cashier to pay his share of the bill. Roddy followed.

"You sure do look like my nephew, Corey, Roddy," he said again. Roddy smiled and turned away trying to end the engagement with this man without being rude. For that he was proud of himself. He could have made a nasty remark. He thought about mentioning the flood but caught himself in time to avoid a fifteen minute description of the event, not that he wasn't interested, but not interested enough to hear this man tell it. Out they went, the two boys, thankful for the advice and the door through which to escape.

They found a campsite along the river that seemed almost too low to support fish, except for what appeared to be deep pools through which water trickled in and out. It was dry, no doubt about it, and had been for some time. But there were fish, panfish, sunnies, no trout, but sunnies would do. They snapped up the worms they dug up from a grassy patch under an oak tree, so that they had enough fish for lunch. But no firewood. They hadn't thought to stop for some. All they needed was a few sticks that would burst into flame in these arid conditions. They found a few, mostly birch twigs and small branches that one swing of a hatchet could cut down to size.

Marty brought out the cook kit with skillet and tin cups for water that they brought in a five gallon jug. Roddy opened a can of Boston baked beans and nestled it up against the would-be fire in the designated fire pit and Marty buttered the pan. No one around. Late Sunday afternoon and weekend campers had packed up and gone home. No smoldering fires, just waste bins filled with trash that some county employee would probably come by in the morning to pick up. Quiet, a slight breeze and a three-man pup tent beside which they positioned two canvas folding chairs. 'Twas good, so good. Ten sunnies, twenty little filets, easily carved out and prepared with Shore lunch, and two Cokes to wash down the fish and beans.

Roddy struck the match and the two boys watched the twigs burst into flame. A few more twigs, then sticks, and a couple of branches from a birch and an oak, enough for their short term fire. They would not sit long by firelight that night, not long because of the lack of wood and the swarm of mosquitoes that recognized a surprise Sunday evening feast. Insect repellent was not an option because the smell lingered through the night, clung to sleeping bags, and greased their skins like cooking oil, and felt as if they were wrapped in plastic seal. Forget the dope, eat, prop themselves inside the tent and talk. Talk, about what?

Marty opined about the diversity of the physical world, an environment providing insects for the birds, fish for the egrets, and helpless humans for mosquitoes. Roddy considered the contours of land and rivers for exploration and challenge, an opportunity to prove oneself against natural forces, test one's metal so to speak. Not much challenge here. For Marty the challenge was academic. He had applied for admission to several colleges including Carlton and Hamlin, hoping to be accepted in one or the other and reap the benefits of both. His grade point and test scores could compete, but did his family have the finances combined with the college support to make it happen? He hoped out loud and Roddy listened as if from another planet, having no such credentials and frankly little interest.

Instead Roddie wanted to fly, at least metaphorically, from world to world to learn by experience, experience that might begin here by a nearly dried up river in a campground cooking fish over a campfire with Marty. He always found his time with Marty stimulating even though he came from a different world, sort of, if you think of his academics. But they could still talk to one another on important matters. They could muse, project, even relax in moments of silence. Time with Roddy was now time. His future had more to do with Jason, whom he had not yet seen but seemed an extension of Darrell, he hoped not in disability but in commitment and understanding.

But how long can two boys talk inside a three man tent without feeling the encompassing arms of Morpheus gather them up and cradle them in sleep. Sometime in the night, Roddy dreamed, at first a vague disconnected series of leaps from hardware store to biking along Lake Minnetonka to coming to rest on the startling image of him flicking lighted matches at his sister and her yelling "Stop it" and he laughing until her blouse caught fire and the tongues of flame leaped up to her hair surrounding her face in a hideous aura that poured down upon her eyebrows and lashes until she was devoured in flame. He heard himself scream and sat up. Marty propped himself on his elbows. Roddy struggled for breath hyperventilating as he tried to clear his mind.

"You ok?"

"I feel heat. There's fire. Here. Look." He pointed through the tent wall toward a flicker of light, Marty unzipped the tent and peered out. A wind had come up to fan flames from the west end of the campground where a few hours earlier the last campers had made their weekend home.

"Holy shit. This place is on fire. We've got to scram. Now. Call 911." Marty bolted from the tent, grabbed pots and pans, the hatchet and through them in the Prius trunk while Roddy pulled the sleeping bags from the tent and threw them unrolled into the back seat. The heat intensified. The tent might have to stay. No, pull the stakes, collapse it and throw into the car. Go. Now. But the fire left only a tunnel surrounded by flame through which they could escape. No, if they tried that exit, the car could explode with them in it. To the river, one of the deep pools and hope they could survive until rescued. They clung to each other in water up to their necks when sitting, dunking their heads to keep cool and flameproof.

"Is this what you mean by adventure?" Marty jibed.

"Not quite."

"Was it the fire you sensed that made you scream?"

"Yes, in a way, but no, I didn't sense the forest aflame until I saw the flicker through the tent wall."

"So what made you scream?"

The heat was becoming so intense the boys kept their heads under water longer, hoping burning branches wouldn't fall on them. There was no place to go. Then the BOOM. The Prius was a ball of fire thirty yards from them. They still had a chance if the river didn't boil them.

"We've got to get out of here." Marty yelled in a panic to escape. He started to climb up the river bank, but Roddy pulled him back.

"No we don't. We can't. We have to wait. That's our only chance." Roddy sat him down farther into the river and somewhat deeper.

So they sat. The fire roared over them and around them, branches crackled, leaves and twigs fell beside them and hissed upon the water, raising its temperature. If this went on much longer they would die. All they could do was wait and hope. While they waited Roddy thought about the nightmare that had awakened him in time to avoid the flaming peril that now surrounded them. The image of his sister's burning face crackled in his mind like the fire outside. Was this some kind of retribution for his secret sins? Was the universe looking for ways to torment him even kill him until he confessed? Was this God giving him a prelude to the fiery symphony of hell? He deserved this, but Marty didn't. How could God do this to Marty? Again it came down to justice if there was such a thing.

A bull horn blared? "Is anybody in there?"

The boys could see nothing, but yelled as loud as they could. "We're in the river. We're in the river. Help! Help!"

"Stay where you are. We'll find you."

Now the boys could see the streams of water gushing over the trees, still not close to them but slowing the flames. They waited. A tree crashed a few feet from them dropping burning branches into the river raising the water temperature a few degrees. It was like a steam bath now, too hot to keep eyes open, too hot to see.

"We're over here. Over here." They each kept screaming hoping their voices were loud enough to be heard over the roar of water and flame.

They heard the truck before they saw it spraying water from its several hoses as it plunged through the burning trees, followed by another and an ambulance with blaring siren tracking behind its fire engine sentries.

"Cut the sirens," someone yelled. "Listen, listen."

The boys were hoarse from yelling and from the smoke now settling in around them stinging eyes and throat. It was harder to breathe, even to gasp for air. As they clung to each other, Marty slipped below the surface, Roddy pulled on him to stay up, and dragged him to the river bank for him to hold on to. He succeeded with Roddy's weakening support.

The firemen listened but could only hear the roar of hoses on hissing foliage. They saw the charred husk of Prius and found no one inside. The air around them was clearing enough for them to see the river. One of the men suspected that if the boys were alive, that's where they'd be. "Come," he demanded as four men ran to the river bank. There they saw one boy with head above water clinging to the bank and another face down beside him. The men splashed to them and dragged and carried them to shore where they began CPR on the one and attached oxygen to the other who at first resisted then succumbed to the gentle air clearing his lungs. The paramedics placed both boys on stretchers and slid them into the ambulance and drove through the now open corridor. The search continued for other possible victims and an attempt to locate the start of the fire apparently on the west end of the campground, the direction from which the wind came. The fire proceeded along the river forest downstream followed by hoses blasting water in pursuit. More trucks arrived from the east end and drowned the flames that now subsided to a fuming mass of hot smog rising over them and swirling off to the east.

On the Rochester news, reporters showed videos from a helicopter of the flaming area that they announced covered about 200 acres including two farm buildings but no houses in the path. The initial report as to the cause of the fire was a careless camper who neglected to completely douse his campfire, followed by a warning sent out by the Department of Natural Resources about containing campfires during the draught coming up short of banning them altogether. Two boys, one white and one apparently Hispanic, they announced, were taken to the Mayo Clinic to be treated for smoke inhalation, burns and trauma. Neither seemed to be in critical condition. Neither boy had ID on his person and none was found in the ashes of tent and automobile, but the car license plate would provide that information soon.

Roddy lay half awake with oxygen mask over his nose and IV in his left arm. He struggled to awaken from the image of Julia on fire and the flames swirling around him and Marty as they submerged themselves in the pool. He believed he was alive, because his face and arms burned and all he could taste and smell was smoke. He opened his smarting, teary eyes and realized he was surrounded in white: sheets, walls, pillow and now a woman who stood beside him at his high bed.

"Where am I? Where's Marty? Is he okay? He begged in near panic.

"He's fine in the bed on the other side of the curtain," she soothed. "Your in the Mayo Clinic."

"Can I talk to him?"

"Not yet. He's still asleep. We don't want to wake him. We've contacted your parents who will be arriving soon. Here's a couple of eye drops to make your eyes feel better. You're going to be just fine."

"My skin hurts."

"You have some miner burns from the heat like a severe sunburn. We've put a light coating of salve on your arms, neck and face to ease the discomfort and prevent infection."

"How did we get here?"

"The ambulance responded to an emergency call, yours, no doubt."

Roddy closed his eyes and let the drops assuage the sting. Images from the fire and his imagination commingled in confusion that left him wondering what was real and unreal. He felt guilty as if he had started the fire. He lit the matches for the campfire, but the forest fire came from the west. Still it seemed the two garages and the old barn fire, both of which were his doing, still smoldered enough to catch fire in the rising wind of his imagination. They hadn't threatened him as they did now. Maybe, just maybe, they had burst into flame to warn him he could never completely escape them. But he had escaped the physical fire. It was the mental one that still smoldered.

Julia rushed in and threw her arms around him to his cry of, "Ooooh, that hurts." She pulled herself away with apologies as she gasped at his red face and arms bleeding through the white salve. And there stood his mother and father, Dennis and Carmen, smiling but aghast at his appearance and commiserating with their disbelief that they had nearly lost him. Beside them were Jose and Isabella, Marty's parents who the nurse admonished to wait until their son awakened which was now happening.

"Where am I? Why are you here?" Marty heard their voices.

The nurse pulled back the curtain so that they could view Marty, like Roddy, plugged in the respirator and IV. His parents, having seen Roddy, were prepared for the sunburnt image of their son, who was groggy with sleep and sedative.

"All I can smell is smoke." He coughed."

"mi Hijo, mi Hijo, lo siento, te amo." She stopped herself realizing that she should offer comforting words and let him sleep. "El doctor dijo que puedo venir a casa con nosotros esta tarde. Duerma ahora."

That was Isabella, who added for the benefit of the others, "We see you at three."

"We want to hear all about it, but not now. You need more sleep. Besides you can't talk with that mask over your nose." That was Carmen with a lilt in her voice.

"You came together?" Roddy, surprised and delighted, pulled the oxygen mask to the side to speak and without waiting for an answer addressed Julia. "It's so good to see you," as if she was the one with the near death experience. Tears came to his eyes that the guests thought were the aftermath of smoke.

But Julia looked at him strangely knowing there was more to his particular address to her than the words said. "It's good to see you safe," she said.

"Sorry about the matches," he mumbled through the mask.

What did he mean? She tried to imagine what meanderings his mind was taking and how he had arrived at that apology. Then she realized he must be thinking about the lit matches he had thrown at her. Was that it? What did they have to do with the fire that nearly took his life? This was not the time to ask.

"It's time to go," Dennis announced. "We'll be back about 3."

They said their goodbyes and for Roddy to get some rest and how sorry they were that it happened and how glad they were that they would be okay. "We're very lucky," Roddy uttered in response to which Dennis said, "I'd say blessed." And closed the door.

"Blessed. . . Blessed," Roddy let the word sink in. Maybe he was blessed. He had escaped prosecution for two crimes of arson and now escaped death by the same means he had committed those crimes. Blessed, maybe charmed or more likely haunted. What would it take for the phoenix to rise from the ashes?

CHAPTER THIRTEEN

THREE DAYS LATER JASON was transported from the VA Hospital to the Johnson home on the north side of Willow pond on Perch Street in Paradise Heights. He lay in a hospital bed with a rise and fall push-button efficiency for easy in and out procedures. Roddy, now carless and nearly recovered from the life threatening experience mounted his bike and rode west the two miles to the Johnson home where he would finally meet Jason, the man he wanted to meet for so many reasons he couldn't count them. It was early afternoon so the Johnsons had not left for the bakery yet and Angela was out with her girlfriends. They greeted Roddy with a hug and commiseration for the trauma he had experienced and were so thankful that he and his friend were safe which Roddy acknowledged had been scary, then changed the focus to Jason.

"May I see him?"

"Of course, he's in the back bedroom about ready for his therapy that Pete puts him through. He's coming along fine."

"So what happened to him?"

"He can tell you. Go down the hall. It's on the left."

The door was open. Roddy peered in hesitantly in case Jason was sleeping. He was propped up in bed reading sports section of the *Star and Tribune* and shaking his head over another Twins loss. When he saw Roddy in the doorway, he motioned him in.

"You must be Roddy. Angela has told me about you. Some guy, she says. Are you some guy?"

"Some guy, I guess." He felt like a block of wood but the wood moved toward Jason who looked like an Adonis, the male counterpart to Angela's Venus. His bare torso emerged above the sheets exhibiting strong arms, shoulders and pectoral muscles. Roddy was impressed. This was the man "hurt" in Afghanistan, who looked anything but disabled.

"You've had quite a scare I heard, playing with fire, right?" An attempt at humor, perhaps.

"Ya, I guess, but we're okay," referring also to Marty, "but what about you? You don't look like a wounded veteran."

"What do wounded vets look like?"

Roddy was embarrassed to consider Darrell's image to represent all injured vets. "I don't know except for a vet I knew who was homeless and froze to death in the snow last December."

Just in case that wasn't a joke Jason said, "I'm sorry."

"You don't look anything like him. So what happened, or don't you want to talk about it?

Jason frowned and looked at Roddy quizzically as if to assess what Roddy expected of the story he was about to tell, then proceeded, "I was one of four guys and a gal that survived a shelling. Bill caught a bullet in his thigh but managed to drag me under a staircase and call for the medics while the others lay in pieces throughout the room. I was losing blood fast. My left side was a mess and hurt like hell. My leg was useless. Bill stuffed his shirt into the hole left by the outer reach of the grenade that shattered the other lives, trying to stop the bleeding. That's all I remember until I woke up in the medical tent with tubes all over and in me. They told me I was lucky to be alive because I had lost so much blood. If it weren't for Bill impeding the blood flow with his shirt and calling the medics I'd have been a goner. Bill's femur was broken by the bullet, but the surgeons patched him up okay. He's back in his home in Kentucky now. I owe him my life."

"So they patched you up, too."

"Well, ya, they shipped me to Germany first, where the surgeons worked on me. My left kidney had to go. You only need one. And my left hip and leg were shattered. They could removed the kidney and rebuild the hip and leg with titanium, but the muscles were gone. I don't know how and where they got the tissue to rebuild them, but they did, although that's what's taking the most time to mend. I have no strength in that leg. So I was in the German hospital for two weeks until they determined they could send me home to the Minneapolis Vets Hospital. That was a long rough trip. Luckily I could eat and drink, but having to sit up and stretch my legs that were wrapped in an elastic bandage to keep my blood from clotting felt like someone twisting an auger into my side. But I'm home now and recovering. I'm doing fine. I'm one of the fortunate ones.

Roddy listened and observed, apparently trying to determine Jason's mental state. It seemed Jason was quite adjusted and accepting of what happened and his present condition. Or was he simply a good actor, one who knew how to present an all-right face to the world and cover up the agony within. Roddy wondered if he could connect with Jason. Maybe they were worlds apart not like Darrell at all, not like him, Roddy. Maybe Jason was a soldier with a soldier's mind and commitment beyond concern for his own life. Maybe he considered his losses as a part of war and refused to curse his fate.

"The hardest part," Jason continued, "is the death, bloody meaningless death of people you care about, who are the ones who have supported you through the nightmare of war, if not literally hand in hand, then at least in their concern. Gone. Just like that. Gone. No life to live. Loved ones left mourning like me, yes, but more like wives and children that will have to live without them. Grace, Thomas, Juan, and Demetri. They were special people." He stopped and seemed to drift away before he returned with, "I didn't mean to tell you all that. Why did I? I don't know."

"I'm so happy you're safe and so happy to meet you. Angela has told me so much about you." That's all he could think of to say. Jason would understand him and Darrell, he was sure of it now. Jason had inner wounds that needed attending. Roddy wondered if his parents knew that. He would discover more from him as they became good friends.

Pete walked in, all business. "Time to torture you, son."

"I'd better leave." Roddy rose from the lounge chair.

"No, no, you can help if you want. Here, you stand here." He pointed to the head of the bed, "and I'll help him swing his legs out while you take his right arm. Then we'll stand him up. Ready, Jason?"

"Yeah, I suppose. Just take it easy. I don't want my hip to collapse."

"It won't collapse in our company, will it Roddy."

"Are you sure you want my help?" Roddy trembled at the thought of causing a collapse.

"Sure, you'll do fine."

Together they swung his legs out and helped him stand up to his walker. He had no trouble supporting himself with his strong arms, but his left leg appeared quite useless, sort of hung there and shuffled with each step. "Damn that hurts," he muttered but minced his way toward the bedroom door toward the bathroom. That was his first destination, a trying encounter with knee bending to sit and release himself, then to the exercise device he strapped his legs into that rotated his legs for him and that he was supposed to rotate with pressure from his left leg. He did both as required. He would do what was required. He didn't intend to be an invalid long. He would rebuild muscle if it took him a year or more. Roddy could see his determination with each effort. He could learn from this man and maybe Jason would take an interest in him.

CHAPTER FOURTEEN

THE PAIN DIDN'T SUBSIDE with each therapy session. Instead it increased. Something was wrong. The surgeon suspected that his femur was too shattered to accept the titanium ball and spike to fit the metal rebuilt socket. Now the choice was to shorten the leg at least three inches. That was unacceptable because of the further damage it would cause. Or replace the leg with a prosthesis, the only real choice, but one that would with physical and occupational therapy give him mobility and a relatively normal life. A set back, but a circumstance Jason could overcome. It was up to him to climb this mountain.

When Roddy heard the news, he was angry at the surgeon who should have known that the first surgery was pointless and at the circumstances of war that necessitated a man of such physical stature to be reduced to disabled status. It wasn't fair. Roddy felt smoldering ashes inside, smoldering because flames were of no use. He hated feeling helpless and wondered much more how helpless Jason must feel. Jason had a choice: he could curse his fate or determine to be the best prosthetic walker, even runner, on the planet.

Jason chose the latter, not without anger, not without grief, but finally acceptance and determination.

"God dammit, I wanted that leg," he yelled at Roddy. "God dammit, man. I still feel it there even though it's gone. They took it. I signed it away as the only option. Shit. I did it. I let them have it. They showed me a contraption they'd hook up to my hip. Shit. What if my hip collapses? They said it was strong, a piece of steel. They're confident, like the first time.

Shit. Shit. Shit."

Roddy felt the heat burn his face red, but said nothing. What was there to say? He was no counselor. He had no advice to offer. In fact, he might have cursed God and taken his own life, the coward that he felt himself to be. He, Roddy, was no hero, just a burning, vengeful coward, now curious to observe Jason.

"But I'm alive, not underground like my buddies. I'm alive. Why I am and they aren't is a mystery to me, but life doesn't make sense to me at the moment. I don't know why I joined the army or why we were sent to Afghanistan, or what makes our leaders think we can win these wars in hot, mountainous, remote hideaways where insurgents are ready to ambush and cities are infested with vermin waiting to snipe at their enemies, anyone that opposes them, especially us. I don't get it. And here I am in my bed at home with one leg and the other in a machine shop somewhere soon to be delivered, probably an Amazon special."

Roddy laughed, "You still have your sense of humor."

"You think I'm laughing?"

"No, no. I didn't mean it that way. I'm sorry."

"It was kind of funny, an Amazon Special, $2099 or $3559 for the blue tooth that connects to the brain chip for dancing or kicking ass." Now he laughed.

"That one would give you a leg up." Roddy smiled at his own cleverness fully into the lighter moment.

"I'm going to make it, man."

"Of course, you are." But Roddy wasn't so sure. He wasn't so sure if he, Roddy, would make it with two good legs and what about Marty and his parents? How would they make it? How would they pay the ambulance and hospital bills without insurance. The Mayo Clinic experience must have cost thousands. The Martinezes didn't have that kind of money. If you're poor, you get poorer. God damn. He didn't say it, but thought it. It was becoming a part of his perspective of the world. God damn. We're people just for profit?

CHAPTER FIFTEEN

AT AFTERNOON BREAK FROM work Roddy sat at a window table at Pete and Emma's and nibbled at yesterday's blueberry muffin and sipped a latte, a newly acquired taste because it was available and offered free from Emma, dear Emma, who seemed to resonate to Roddy's emotions. This afternoon Roddy had little to say, not too unusual, since he depended on Emma to draw his thoughts from him. But today he was even more pensive after spending time with Jason that morning. He didn't want to express his dismay over the long process Jason faced in first fitting a temporary leg and then a permanent prosthesis after examinations and interviews and calculations of cost that may or may not be covered by the VA. And then the calculations of his monthly disability compensation according to formulae. So depressing, so mechanical, so robotic, it seemed in spite of the counselor with whom Jason felt connected. He didn't want to express his distress over Jason's lifelong disability to Emma who, though cheerful in spirit, had to be deeply distressed herself. And what about Pete, the forever soldier in mind if not in body, proud of his son's sacrifice for his country in spite of Jason's anger with these senseless wars. He believed in his son's fortitude, his athletic prowess, his strength of mind. That was good, encouraging and supportive, but lacked in feeling and understanding of Jason's mind. Emma knew her son better and didn't need Roddy to speak of what she and he felt. Maybe they could sometime later when the procedure had proven positive and Jason was literally on his feet.

Then Angela appeared, just returning from a poetry class she was taking at the Loft Literary Center downtown and sat across from Roddy with her black coffee, no pastry to affect her enticing figure. Just to be in the aura of her smile cheered Roddy. He was drawn to her like the sun draws the moon or maybe in his case an asteroid swirling helplessly in space.

"I want to share a poem with you," she suggested, waiting for acceptance.

"I don't know anything about poetry," Roddy demurred uncomfortably, not wanting for her to embarrass him by having to explain the poem to him.

"Don't worry. I think you'll get it."

He nodded and she began.

Even
After
All this time
The sun never says to the earth,

"You owe
Me."

Look
What happens
With a love like that,
It lights the
Whole
Sky."

Angela couldn't wait to explain.

"I think he is saying that love gives us life. We owe nothing to anyone, not to the creator or our parents or ourselves. Love is the foundation of our lives, the light that frees us. That's what it means to me. What does it mean to you?"

"Yeah, if we have no obligation, we're free, right? I mean if we don't owe even ourselves anything. But what about responsibility to others and for our actions? Isn't he being unreal?"

"You just said it frees us up, right? So if we're free, we're without obligation, we can respond from the heart out of love. Don't you think?

"I guess so. It depends on the heart. But if the heart is snared in anger, does that give us freedom to hate?"

'No, I don't think so. Then we're really not free because we owe something to somebody and we let that obligation drive us to get even."

"I see what you mean. So freedom from not owing, opens the love in us. Is that it?"

"I think so."

"I get it," he beamed, amazed that he had just had a discussion about a poem. "Who wrote that?"

"He went by the name, Hafiz, a Sufi poet from Persia, Iran today, in the 14th century.

"So long ago and still read today."

He gazed at her in admiration, not knowing yet how this poem mattered. He would have to discover that a little at a time. For the moment he felt his muscles relax as if to let down his defenses, just for the moment, and then they tightened again around his heart as if it needed protection. He wasn't sure that the sun was love and that its light was intentional or that its warmth was embracing. He liked the idea, but the notion seemed strained to him. Still he was happy Angela shared it with him. Was it the poem or was it simply an opportunity to share. He liked the latter notion, that she wanted to share what pleased her with him. Maybe to avoid talking about Jason, whose condition was devastating to her. He knew that by her body language when he observed her with him. She was attempting to be strong, attempting to find the light. That, too, could be the reason for her sharing that poem, finding the love in the sun.

He was reminded of his summer school teacher's admonition that he should put his angry ramblings into form and showed him how to write an essay. An essay, how different from the poem he just heard, but language to express something that needed to be said. How different in what needed to be said. What kind of a world did Hafiz live in so many years ago that allowed him such a perspective. The sun shines its love on everything and everybody. He'd have to think about that.

CHAPTER SIXTEEN

AFTER CHRISTMAS EVE EARLY candlelight service with their dad, Roddy and Julia had dinner at the Bergitta's Diner of roast turkey, potatoes and gravy, and dressing with sugar cookies for dessert, after which they spent the night at their dad's condo opening their presents and sleeping in their separate rooms. Julia had saved enough of her allowance to buy her dad a pair of furry slippers and Roddy an acrylic paint kit, while she received a mini pad from her dad and a subscription to *Seventeen* from Roddy. Roddy gave his dad a Pendleton shirt that cost him more than he expected to pay but it was the least he could do after his dad's generosity. Their father gave them each tickets to Taylor Swift concert at Xcel Center in St. Paul in mid-January. Christmas Day with Carmen and Roger, not Cliff, openly Roger and never Cliff, was also pleasant and generous. Roger gave $50 to each and their mom gift certificates at Best Buy plus a late afternoon dinner with her parents whom they hadn't seen for nearly the whole year and felt a bit awkward.

The winter seemed to stretch on interminably for Roddy who made up his mind that he would go to school as required and try to do the assignments no matter how inane they seemed to be. He took his English class more seriously than before, because he was fascinated by stories that others had told in a compelling way and the poetry that seemed to well up in the poet and spill out on the page.

He seemed to be going through the motions, a survival mode, until he could think of his next move. His time with his mother was more comfortable. She seemed to accept him, not fight with him, not make demands, just let him be in a casual way as if there had never been antagonism between them. And he liked Roger, her boyfriend, who worked as a system analyst in an auto shop. What brought them together was Roddy's need for a car after his Prius had burned. Roger took in an old VW beetle that needed some repair, but was fixupable and suggested that the two of them could restore it to good running order for little money. Maybe Roger was just trying to win him over, but to Roddy it appeared he really cared about him and liked working on cars. Besides the two of them could make a nothing into a good something. Why not? And so they did. But who was Roger? His dad had flinched when Julia had said Roger instead of Cliff and his dad said they knew each other in high school. What was that all about? Maybe he'd find out some day, but not now.

The sun isn't always the lover Hafiz suggested. "Sometimes too hot the eye of summer shines." He learned that in English class from a Shakespearean sonnet. He couldn't believe he remembered it, but it had something to say about his musings. The sun can burn; it can scorch and parch and kill. Yes, the sun provides its warmth and light for all life, but people die in the desert and many people live each day under the nurturing sun only to starve to death. And what about Darrell and Jason? One dead and one crippled with his only fault that he signed up for war? Does the sun really care? He doubted it. He doubted that the sun had any concern about anything: it just went about its business of rising and setting as the world turns (not just a soap opera on tv). The sun's nature was to do its thing with no regard for anything. He wouldn't share those thoughts with Angela. She might not get it.

In the meantime, Jason struggled with one leg and a hip in and out of a wheelchair waiting for his surgical wound to heal enough for the fitting of a prosthesis. Not much to do but observe the sun rise and set, watch tv and read. He perused the *Star Tribune* each morning, first the editorials and letters to the editor that often commented on the Trump campaign challenging the stalwarts of the Republican Party. Trump called Ted Cruz a liar and Jeb Bush a pansy or something of that sort, posturing himself as the man who could get things done for the common people and to "Make America Great Again." Jason liked his swagger, his confident, know-it-all posture that belittled the stagnant Republican Party. Maybe this man could break the stalemate of Congress, create a better healthcare plan and jobs for the many unemployed workers abandoned by technological advances. He paid attention to the liberal counterpoint that tried to discredit Trump for his demeaning words about women. That he didn't like, but nobody's perfect. If he could get the job done. . . He made plans to travel to Eau Claire, Wisconsin for the Trump rally in early April. He needed a chauffeur.

CHAPTER SEVENTEEN

THE SOMETIMES UNLOVING sun poured its early warmth on the mid-March morning raising the temperature into the 40's and promising a comfortable 55 degrees, a temperature that shed winter coats and invited noonday walks in city parks and trails. Spring was here after a mild winter that for many proved the truth of climate change and for others meant a natural flux in weather patterns that happened in cycles. Whatever the persuasion, it was a day for smiles, pleasant greetings and generosity. Roddy's father, however, sat staring through the newspaper at the breakfast table as if to see beyond its stories, seemingly recreating his own from the days gone by. At least that's what Roddy thought as he gently inquired, "What's wrong, Dad?"

"What makes you think something is wrong?" His father retorted somewhat agitated at being discovered.

"You seem a bit down this beautiful morning."

"Well, maybe."

"What's going on?" Dare he ask?

"I was just thinking about what your mother and I used to do on beautiful spring mornings like this, how I'd open the shop late and we'd spend time together and go out to breakfast after a walk and feel the spring air warm our spirits."

"You still miss her."

"I guess I do. I loved her once."

"But?"

"Yeah, but…"

"But what?"

"But by noon we were at each other's throats over something. It didn't matter what. It was no use. It was my fault. You and Julia got caught in the middle."

"Yeah, I know. We're all better off, don't you think?"

"I don't know. I guess so. Sometimes it doesn't feel like it."

"I know. We did have some good family times, especially on camping trips and at the lake."

"You remember."

"I remember. I remember how you took me fishing and how you taught me to filet sunnies and bass and northerns, how to shimmy the knife along the rib cage to produce five boneless filets. I loved that."

"Me, too. Maybe we can go fishing again soon."

"I'd like that."

"I don't hate your Mom, you know."

"No, I don't either. She's my mom, but I never know where I stand with her."

"Or with me?"

"I can't believe we're talking."

"I want you to be happy. Hey, the sun's shining. Let's go for a walk and eat at Bergitta's Diner."

"Thanks, Dad, but it's Friday. I have school."

"That never stopped you before."

Roddy bit his tongue to prevent a comeback remark. The congenial moment had passed. Things were normal again, tense, iffy, on the edge.

"I'll see you this afternoon at the store. Bye."

Roddy shut the door behind him proud of himself for not responding to his dad's reminder of his truancies. Maybe his dad didn't mean it as a dig. Maybe it was actually a compliment. Yes, he would take it as such as he climbed into his Blue Beetle, the replacement for the burnt Prius that Roger and he had refurbished. He felt a pang as he thought about how fun that was with his mother's boyfriend. God damn his life was complicated. Better not to feel things. Then he thought of Angela.

Maybe he could make it through school. If he passed his courses, he'd be only two credits short. He could graduate with his class if he promised to pass make-up summer courses. He'd be a high school graduate, a goal that had never seemed important to him until now. At Pete and Emma's, Angela had another Hafiz poem to share. Okay, he'd listen and hope it made more sense than the last one.

She seemed to bloom like a rose opening as she leaned toward him across the table and as if offering him a whiff of her fragrance. He was ready for anything she had to offer, her smile, stories, her poems. She said, "Listen."

> God
> Disguised
> As a myriad things and
> Playing a game
> Of tag
>
> Has kissed you and said,
> "You're it—
>
> I mean, you're Really IT!"
> "Now

It does not matter
What you believe or feel

For something wonderful,

Major-league Wonderful
Is someday going
To

Happen."

She paused as if in devotion, still smiling, then looking at him, dead center into him.

"What do you think?"

"I don't know."

"You're it. You're Really IT. Don't you see?"

He didn't know what he felt except that it was good, good to hear her reciting, to hear her say, "You're it," to feel that he mattered. To her. To God, maybe.

"Thank you. I like that. I hope it's true."

"It is true. You have to believe it. Believe it."

"I'll try. . . My dad and I had a real conversation this morning. I think we sort of connected. He's lonely. He still thinks of Mom. He needs someone. I think he really cares about me. He wants me to be happy. I want that for him, too. I don't know what to do with my feelings." He caught himself gushing.

"I'm happy for you and your dad. Just let the feelings come. Let them come." She reached out and touched his hand. A warmth spread through him completely different from the heat he had so often experienced in anger. This warmth was completely new to him, welcome and frightening. He took her hand in response, thanked her, and rose. "I have to get to work. Dad's expecting me. See you tomorrow?"

"I think I can arrange that." She blew him a kiss.

CHAPTER EIGHTEEN

HE CALLED MARTY SATURDAY morning in late March, said he needed to talk, about so much. "I'll pick you up."

"I still feel like I've smoked a pack of cigarettes, eyes still burn and throat feels raw, Marty commented over the phone.

"Really? I'm back to normal. No, I'm better than normal."

"Part of it is all the talking I've been doing working on the Bernie Sanders campaign."

"Really?" He said it again and waited for another surprise. "Let's talk. I'll pick you up. We'll go to the park."

They found a table with benches across from one another, picked at blueberry muffin and sipped a macchiato from Dunn Brothers while spewing out events of the past few weeks. After recounting their near death experience in the forest fire, the hospital stay, the pending bills that Marty's family were negotiating so far with little success, Roddy oozed over his relationship with Angela and her poems that left him confused, eager, stimulated, thoughtful, maybe in love and Marty more subdued confessed that he had growing affections for Juanita who was working with him on the Sanders campaign, making phone calls to the Latino population, writing letters about the dangers of Trump or any of those Republican candidates, especially for Latinos and all people of color, organizing, raising money.

Roddy was impressed and a bit confused. He knew Jason was a Trump supporter who hoped he'd launch a political bomb

The Stranger Who Was Himself

that would blow up the two parties with their feet embedded in concrete. He was sure his dad was for Hillary Clinton, but he wasn't clear about where his mom and Roger stood. He hadn't really talked to Angela about politics and as for him, Roddy, he had no idea. He agreed with Jason that the military and especially the veterans were in dire need of federal money and that Trump made that issue a major part of his campaign. So the dialogue began. Who was Bernie Sanders anyway? Roddy said he planned to take Jason to the Trump rally on April 2 to hear the man in person and offer support. Did Marty want to come along?

"No, Thank you. Do you know his history?" Marty pointed out Trump's failed casinos, his default on payments to contractors, his demeaning remarks about women, and especially his verbal attacks on Mexican illegal aliens and immigrants. "We're all criminals and rapists, you know."

Roddy didn't know. "Jason says Trump spouts off but really doesn't mean those things. He's just trying to rile up the people to see that he wants to put America first. We can't keep giving jobs away and threatening the lives of our people."

"So you believe Mexicans threaten the lives of our people?"

"Some of them do, I guess."

"How about the white guys who massacre kids at Sandy Hook Elementary or the white racist that shoots six black people in an African church in Charleston and the gang warfare. I don't think immigrants are the problem. Look at me. Am I a problem?"

"Well, no, of course not, but you're different."

"So I'm different. That must mean that you know several Latinos who are not at all like me, that are dangerous people preying on white society. Is that it?"

"Well, no, I don't know that."

"So you don't know what you're talking about."

"I don't know what to think."

"That's a start."

The steam rising from the two boys evaporated as they paused to catch a breath of morning air, realizing they were at odds for the first time in their relationship. The two had always learned from each other. Could that still happen? Marty was clearly agitated and Roddy felt accused. It's true he didn't know what he was talking about. He was relying on the little information he had from Jason whom he respected and whom he had promised a ride to the Trump rally. He would go. Why shouldn't he? It's a free country and he said so to Marty to which Marty replied, "Let's keep it free. Let's vote for our people, not for the guy who flaunts a lot of ill-gotten money."

That was the end of the conversation. No more talk about Juanita and Angela or about Roddy's discussion with his dad. Trump had already built a wall between them and both boys felt it. They parted company much sooner than anticipated, Marty claiming he had schoolwork and Roddy that he had to go to work, each suspecting the other was less than honest. They intended to do a spring campout soon but made no plans.

In truth, Roddy and Julia were slated to spend the weekend with his mother and Roger in a cabin on Lake Superior, an adventure he looked forward to. He liked talking to Roger about cars and mechanics because he felt he had learned a lot from the hardware business and his mom seemed to pay some attention to him because of Roger. When he said something, Roger listened. Consequently, so did his Mom. Soon it became clear that they were Trump supporters but not fanatic. They hoped he'd get the nomination because they couldn't stand Cruz or Jeb Bush for totally different reasons. And Carson looked like he was asleep. They usually voted Democrat but they didn't trust Clinton and didn't want socialist Sanders. Roddy kept his mouth shut. He was getting better at that. They had a good time, hiking up Gooseberry Falls trails, driving up to Grand Maria's and Nannaboujou Lodge for lunch and listening to the Belfast Cowboys sing Irish tunes and Van Morrison songs along the dock as the sun sprayed its last golden rays over the glistening inland sea toward the eastern sky. Roddy fell asleep thinking that maybe if Trump were president, Darrell might have been able to get financial support for better treatment and a more comfortable life, if he were still alive.

Clearly, Marty and Juanita had become an item as they worked on Sander's campaign with their friends Julio, Pablo and Alicia. For the time being Roddy and Marty were traveling in different circles. Roddy, in particular, was focused on Jason who traveled daily to Courage Center where he engaged in physical therapy to build his strength in his upper body and one leg while he continued to wait for the results of studies that would determine if and when he would get a prosthesis that would afford self-propulsion. The first studies were not promising since his whole leg was gone up through the hip that had to be rebuild to provide a method of attachment and the necessary distribution of nerves that would tie his brain to the artificial limb. Evidently, the technocrats would need to create a new device so far eluding them. The hopeful news was that his pelvis was still intact. So Jason kept working and cursing and hoping as he wheeled himself from room to room and down the makeshift ramp to the car for a journey here and there. It wasn't the life he wanted, but it was his life and he decided he would live it.

Roddy visited him often and sometimes drove him to therapy and even worked out a bit at the Center which the personnel there allowed. He was impressed with the attention Jason received from very skilled staff and how accommodating they were to his chauffeur. Roddy built muscle while Jason built confidence. He knew it mattered if he were strong for rehab, if and when the prosthesis was fitted.

CHAPTER NINETEEN

ON APRIL 2, RODDY ROSE to a chilly, cloud-covered day ready as promised to journey east with Jason to the Trump rally. Jason was eager to support Trump having read the news that he was lagging behind Ted Cruz who was recently endorsed by Wisconsin Gov. Scot Walker. Trump, however, had stated that his campaign was strong, that Cruz couldn't be trusted, even lying while holding the Bible above his head. Jason had to hear Trump himself since he believed the news media covered him unfairly. Certainly the Republicans were trying to destroy him in favor of anybody else running for their presidential nominee. Roddy arrived at the Johnson doorstep at 10 a.m and assisted Jason from wheelchair into his Blue Beetle that he sometimes called Moon Rover because when driving he seemed to be circling the earth or at least had that sense of freedom. Emma had packed a lunch for both of them so that they wouldn't have to spend money on junk food. Of course she would surprise them with a bakery offering. They scuttled east on 394 to 94 past St. Paul and Woodbury, through Hudson and on to Eau Claire, truly scuttled because each attempt at gaining speed languished with the automobile's reluctance. The VW had no vigor, no determination, but rose to each acceleration with resigned acceptance, then cruised along at 70 mph as if asleep. If braking were necessary, recalcitrance returned. But they arrived at Memorial High School to a sunny 30 degree afternoon in time to find a parking space in the student lot and meander through the crowds of people who carried signs sporting slogans like "Make America Great Again" and "Vets for Trump" and "Save our Jobs". Jason held up his own cardboard placard with the words "What about Me?" that Roddy had scrawled across it in black letters.

Roddy wheeled Jason in through the back doors of the gymnasium and parked him in the aisle about 20 rows from stage as he took his place beside him and waited and waited while Trump boosters initiated chants, Trump, Trump, Trump. Cruz No, Trump Yes, and whatever else they could come up with to inspire the crowd. Roddy felt as if an open-mouthed monster was about to swallow him whole. He had never been to such an event where people whipped themselves into a frenzy as if in a Pentecostal Church, shouting and yelling to assure Trump's nomination. He and Jason hadn't said much about the upcoming event on the way down, only that they were excited and looking forward to it. But they did talk, at first about the drive, the sluggish VW, and the amenable weather. After all it could be snowing or sleeting to make a nightmare of driving. Then Jason lamented about the loss of his once athletic body that played Hopkins football. He was a great linebacker if he did say so himself. Not any more. No Racquet ball, no skiing, not even any golf, to which Roddy replied, "Maybe, skiing and golf. He saw a game show on TV in which one of the contestants had an artificial limb and ran 10 mile races and played golf."

"Ya but, just a ya but, he probably didn't have his whole leg up to his hip amputated. That's a problem that may be insurmountable."

"Ya but, I can say it, too. You don't know that it is. You're a fighter. I've worked out with you. I watched your determination. Somehow you and the technicians will find a way."

The Stranger Who Was Himself

Roddy couldn't believe his own words, how he was the one looking to a positive future when he was so down from Darrell's troubles and demise and his hatred of war and the politicians that brought young men and women to it. He was offering encouragement, he, with no apparent future for himself, failing school, a hot headed, angry kid with Marty as his only true friend, who had argued him into a corner over his interest in Trump. On the other hand, he was talking with his father now, he liked his mom's new boyfriend and she seemed to pay some attention to him. In fact, he was passing his classes in school, but the flames of his indiscretions still haunted him, sometimes in his dreams, almost like post traumatic events. He was no soldier. He had no wounds except those he had inflicted on himself. Now he was encouraging Jason, amazed at himself.

While they waited, the two companions tore open their brown lunch bags and chomped on a ham and cheese on pumpernickel ryes, an apple, two carrots and a blueberry muffin. Roddy wouldn't have requested pumpernickel, but the lunch was healthy, remarkably tasty and filling.

As they discarded their empty bags in the recycle bin, the gymnasium door swung open and in walked several men and a woman leading the golden haired, or was it orange, Donald Trump in dark suit and red tie. He waved as he climbed the few stairs to the stage platform prepared for him and his entourage that included the mayor but no governor or congressman. Trump was a maverick and that's what attracted Jason.

And he began the gospel according to Trump. He said he's winning. He said Cruz keeps saying how he's beating Trump. He's not. Kasich gives bad speeches, terrible, but he gets good press. Trump doesn't get good press, only the bad stuff, but Trump is a winner in business, in foreign affairs, in smarts.

He's smarter than all of the candidates and tougher. You got to be tough and smart, he says. He's going to build a wall and Mexico is going to pay for it to keep the rapists and criminals out. He's going to make America great again in trade and the military. He's going to support our veterans, defeat ISIS, make the NATO countries pay their share. NATO's obsolete. It doesn't fight terrorism. It doesn't know how. He does. He's going to put America first. He's going to make America a winner.

Roddy listened. What he heard was that Trump would support our veterans like Darrell and Jason. Things could be different if Trump could defeat the terrorists and Americans wouldn't have to send its soldiers into harms way. Maybe he could protect American jobs, too. What about small businesses like his dad's hardware store? The business hadn't been going so well with Home Depot and Menards close by. Dennis was feeling the pinch, needed tax breaks. Maybe Trump could help, get the economy moving. He didn't know if the economy wasn't moving. He only knew what he had just heard. Jason seemed enrapt in Trump's confidence, convinced, it appeared, that he could get done what he promised. Roddy had never doubted that America was a great country. Suddenly Trump was saying it wasn't and he would make it great. Roddy wondered what to say to Jason on the way home. He thought about Marty's disdain and fear of this man he had just heard speak, especially what he said about Mexicans.

On the way home under cloudy sky but clear road in just below freezing weather the VW performed as expected keeping pace with the traffic but not ready to show any initiative. To Jason it didn't matter. He glowed in the aftermath of his champion's proclamations. Roddy, too, admitted that he liked Trump's swagger, his conviction that he could accomplish what previous politicians like Bush and Obama and all those running for the Republican candidacy failed and would fail to do, especially his supposed Democratic opposition, lying Hillary, and socialist buffoon Sanders. There was an anger in Trump that took no prisoners and stirred the fire in Roddy whose embers lay smoldering for some time now but only needed a catalyst to flame up. Trump could be that catalyst if somehow Roddy could explain his allegiance to his friend, Marty. Then again he wouldn't have to explain it. He was too young to vote so it didn't matter. He didn't even have to think about it. And Trump was not the nominee, not yet. Ted Cruz was leading while John Kasich, Jeb Bush, Ben Carson, and Ron Paul were fading into political oblivion. So Roddy listened to Jason pour praises on Trump all the way home with reluctant admiration. He wondered how Pete and Emma and especially Angela would take to Jason's enthusiasm. Silence, Roddy decided, was the best course accompanied with agreeable smiles.

CHAPTER TWENTY

AS THEY APPROACHED 1915 Orchard Ave N, Jason's home, Roddy noticed the police car parked in the driveway. "What the hell?" Jason muttered. In the driveway Roddy flipped his driver's seat forward and pulled out Jason's wheelchair to the silence that hung in the air over the heads of the neighbors to the south that were looking their way from the sidewalk. Before Jason could slide out of his seat onto the wheelchair, a police woman emerged from the Johnson front door and descended the three steps next to the makeshift ramp that Jason in wheelchair would ascend.

"What happened?" Jason questioned with tremor in his voice.

"Your father was in an auto accident," the officer announced, visibly distraught. She waited for the words to sink in.

"Is he hurt bad?"

She nodded.

"Will he be okay?"

"No," she said now with tears in her eyes.

"He's not dead."

She nodded.

"Oh, my God. Oh, my God, what happened? Where's Mom? Angela? Are they okay?"

"Yes, they're in the house."

Roddy stood behind the wheelchair petrified. Not Pete, no not Pete. This couldn't happen.

"Push," Jason yelled. And Roddy pushed up the incline into the house where his mother ran to him crying and Emma, too, with arms around his neck, sobbing. Pete had been their rock, the soldier, always the soldier, who could win every battle with such grace and courage, the one who kept Jason from despair with his unceasing encouragement and exercise routine, the one who encouraged Angela to finish her college education and to write poetry. Now what? And here stood Roddy accompanied by the police woman, who offered her condolences and suggested to Roddy that he leave the family to themselves and their grief. That made sense. In tears he followed the officer out and asked what happened. She said that Mr. Johnson returning from Byerlys had slowed to make a right turn on Duluth St from driving south on Winnetka when a drunk driver, drunk at 5 p.m. in the afternoon plowed into the back of his car at full speed. When the ambulance arrived, the paras pronounced Mr. Johnson dead at the scene, apparently from a broken neck. The drunk driver, not wearing a seatbelt, flew through his windshield and now lay in the hospital in comatose critical condition.

Roddy sat in his car, sat, with nowhere he wanted to go, with no one he wanted to talk to, maybe Marty, but he would have to cross bridges to do that. His mom, but she didn't know Pete Johnson, his dad, yes, it had to be his dad, but not yet. So he sat, alone, stewing about the perfect family broken, no sun lighting up the sky for the well-being of this family, just the indifferent sun that let Darrell freeze to death in the snow, that let his mother and father quarrel themselves into a divorce while he, Roddy, struggled to make sense of his two worlds, now maybe three, short credits and no future prospects. Yes, Jason, what the goddamn hell?

His dad had to know. He and Pete had become very good friends as they labored side by side in the separate businesses and his dad many mornings would rise early enough to have coffee and a Johnson baked muffin before the bakery opened to the waiting crowd at eight a.m and his dad prepared for his nine o'clock hardware store opening. His dad had to know and would know what to do, how to help him, Roddy, to know what to do, too. It amazed him that he trusted his dad, that he needed not only to tell him about Pete, but to hear his voice, to help Roddy understand, to help him pray, to find solace in the scriptures. But Pete's death couldn't be God's plan. Was God as indifferent as the sun? He was almost home. How should he tell Dennis, no, his father, his dad?

He just said it outright as he walked in the door even before his dad could query.

"Pete was killed by a drunk driver."

"What? When?"

"Just an hour ago. We found out when I took Jason home."

The explanation was brief. What mattered now was that his dad needed to tend to the Johnsons who needed him.

"Should I come?" Roddy needed his father. "Where's Julia?"

"Of course, come. They need us. She's at dance practice. Jane's mom will bring her home in the morning."

There was nothing to say and neither attempted words, nor did Emma, Jason, nor Angela. They hugged their friends and each other and sat as if sitting would heal them. The neighbors came. It was on the news. How fast news travels, even when it has the facts wrong. Mr. Kotkee said that the driver who hit Pete's car had died. His death ended any need for vengeance or retribution as if either would satisfy or change the outcome. This incident, the blip on the mortal screen had passed. Only the grief and the funeral remained to acknowledge these lives had really happened and the long lasting memories.

Roddy's dad did what he could by being there, so did Roddy. He wished he could talk to Angela, to take her back to their bike ride out to Lake Minnetonka and to lie in the grass beside her in the Hopkins Park away from Jason's injuries and his own secrets. How he wished he could comfort her. How he wished. He needed Marty.

Before he could muster the nerve and energy to call Marty. Marty called him. He had seen the news and knew immediately who this man was. Roddy had talked of the Johnson's often, especially Jason's struggles to heal both physically and mentally and, of course, Angela, who had captured Roddy's imagination. Marty made no inquiry of the Trump rally and Roddy's time with Jason. Rather he put his arms around his friend and said, "I know you'll miss him. I'm so sorry. There's no explanation for why one fine man dies and another survives terminally handicapped while you and I have life and limb and a promising future."

Roddy believed it was true, that in spite of his immigrant status Marty had a promising future. He was smart, could easily get a college degree, but he wasn't so positive about himself. He thought his chances were about as hopeful as a butterfly in a hurricane. Maybe some of them survive. Maybe they know how to find shelter, but could he learn? One thing for sure is that Marty prized him in spite of whatever politics he might have, or because he knew that Roddy had no politics and could be shaped into doing what was right. Not that he expected Roddy to be a pushover. He had had enough debate on their bike and camping trips to know that Roddy had a mind of his own. What he knew for sure was that Roddy cared about people, especially unfortunate people like Darrell and Jason.

That was the foundation on which Roddy was built in spite of family troubles and failures. But for now Marty knew Roddy needed friendship and healing and that meant just hanging out.

"Will you come with me downtown?" Roddy asked with tears in his eyes.

"I don't understand."

"I want to find Gabe."

"Who's Gabe?" Marty studied Roddy quizzically.

"You remember, one of the two men under the bridge after we met Darrell in the old barn, the drunk guy with Shithead."

"And why do you want to find him?"

"I don't know. It's just that I think I let Darrell down. I should have paid attention. He called me his friend."

"He called both of us his friend, remember."

"Ya, but I went back and you didn't. I know you had your own issues to deal with. I don't blame you, but he needed me."

"Roddy, you were a moment in his life. You don't owe him anything.

"I know that, but I felt his loneliness. I'll never forget the way Gabe looked at me at the Celebration of Remembrance where Darrell was honored. He was Gabe's Darrell, too."

"You're making way too much of this, me amigo."

"Vengas conmigo?

"I don't think you want me with you. This is your mission."

"A mission, is it? Maybe it is."

But first the funeral and better weather for biking. He wanted to bike, because he knew the route that found Gabe and Shithead under the overpass and passed the scene of his unsolved crime. He needed some closure, somewhere, some acknowledgement for his concern. Besides what had happened to Pete was more than he could process. The funeral loomed.

He hoped the minister in St John's Lutheran would say the right things, not just Pete at home with Jesus. That may be comforting to some, probably his dad, but not to him. The burning had returned, rising in tongues that singed his insides, but there was nothing to burn and nothing to put the fire out. Go see Gabe. Tell him about the fire. Go.

At the funeral a week after Roddy's sleepless nights, Pastor Jordahl said little about heaven and focused mostly on the Pete's roles as soldier, husband, father and neighbor. Then unexpectedly it was Jason's turn to speak. The pastor and Dennis tried to assist Jason to the lectern, but Jason refused. He wanted to be on the same level as his family and friends, among them his high school teammates, who sat solemnly before him.

He began with praises for his father's service and for his support of him, Jason, who needed his father's courage and determination. He smiled weakly as if he hardly had the strength. Then his countenance darkened, as if a cloud had passed over the stain glass windows that lit the room. "I appreciate my father's support for our armed forces, for his time in the service, for his encouragement for me to enlist. I don't blame him for my condition. But his was a different war, a war with little loss of life for our troops. Iraq and Afghanistan are another story, more like Vietnam, that took 57,000 thousand of our lives and maimed many more. I am one of the maimed that you honor as a hero of war. I am no hero. I'm a man where no man should have been, willing to be there, yes, but not realizing the cost to me and the thousands of others we called the enemy. They had families, too. Many of them are without arms or legs or suffer from post traumatic stress. Where are they in our thoughts? How will they live out the rest of their lives? And why should I be saying these things at my father's funeral? Because of the irony. My dad was a soldier, returned to his family, only to die by the reckless driving of a drunk. Dad, I'm going to go on fighting for all of those who have died too soon, for all of those who have to overcome the impossible, for life, which is the most precious thing we have. I accept that Dad is at peace, but this is the life we know and we have to make it better for everyone." He paused as if waiting for a final statement to arrive. Then decided he had said it and bowed his head. The congregation of a couple of hundred followed suit. After several moments of silence the minister said "Amen." His mother and sister came to him in tears and wrapped their arms around him. Roddy sat numb.

CHAPTER TWENTY-ONE

HE NEEDED TO FIND Gabe. On a warm May late Saturday afternoon just a week after the funeral Roddy mounted his bike and rode east on the accustomed bike trail past the scene of his arson to the overpass where he had first met Gabe and Shithead. Of course Gabe wasn't there. Why should he be? That meeting was nearly a year ago and much had changed, for Gabe too, no doubt. So he biked toward the shelter where Darrell had worked and occasionally stayed and where Gabe had led him to Darrell whom he had pretended not to know. As he biked he held the image of Gabe's face at the Celebration of Remembrance and his nod to affirm that the name Darrell McClellan was the Darrell he knew. That face he had to find. There sitting on a curb just behind the Hennepin Avenue bridge sat Gabe holding up a sign that read, "Give cash. I need a drink." He looked disheveled as usual but not any worse for wear.

Roddy stopped in front of him without a greeting and waited. "Well, if it isn't Asshole. Where ya been? What are ya doing here? "

"I came to see you. Where's Shithead?"

"In that ashcan over there." He pointed to a waste barrel. "With Darrell."

"Darrell's dead."

"Aren't we all."

"Shithead, too?"

"No, just unreliable. He's gone."

"So we're playing the same game, you and I. Let's be honest. Darrell was your friend and so is Shithead."

"I am honest. Can't you read my sign? I tell the truth, not like some guys that say they're homeless with two hungry kids. I tell the truth and people like it. They toss me a dollar or two out the window for me to chase so they can feel good about themselves for helping a poor son of bitch who's too lazy to get a job and drinks himself to death. I'm undeserving but they are generous do-gooders with a charitable spirit to satisfy their Christian need."

"And it works?"

"Look." He opens his bag that contains a pint of Black Velvet and several dollar bills. "So it's your turn to be honest. What do you want with me?"

"I don't know. I just had to see you. Maybe I want you to tell me who I am. Maybe I'm one of those in the trash cans."

"You need a drink."

The warmth of the day was fading with the sun and Gabe said, "Let's go."

"Where?"

"To my place."

Roddy walked his bike along side Gabe as he led the way. He stopped at a liquor store in the Riverside shopping area to replenish his supply of Black Velvet and then at Whole Foods for two sandwiches, one for each of them. On they walked toward the river, down along the rushing water of the Mississippi filled to the brim with runoff from the north heading south to Louisiana as if on a mission. They came to a stand of trees, willows, Roddy guessed, that provided a shelter from the view of passers by and plopped down on a sleeping bag and blankets that had become the night's lodging for this homeless man, who seemed content with his way of life. Gabe opened the bottle of booze and handed the bottle to Roddy, who rejected it with a wave of his hand.

"So what are you here for?" Gabe studied Roddy.

"I don't know. First, Darrell died in a snowdrift, then just a month ago Jason, my friend, came home from Afghanistan all busted up with an amputated hip, then his dad was killed in an auto accident, and I burned down that old barn that was Darrell's musing place and I'm all screwed up. "He grabbed the bottle and took a swig. His eyes teared as much from dismay as from the liquor that was anything but velvet. He took another.

"You did that?" He broke into laughter. "And they didn't catch you?" He laughed so hard the tears came. Then silence, sudden, dark silence.

No more words, just swigs, just musings, just being for the moment in the presence of the other. Some other. Did it matter who? He had no idea who Gabe was other than the guy who knew Darrell, nothing about why he was homeless and drunk. Gabe handed him the bottle and he took another swig

"Who are you?" Roddy's question.

"A teacher in love with a student who was in love with me. The family didn't prosecute, but I lost my job."

"Oh, my God. Then what?"

"Does it matter?"

"What happened?"

"It's a short story but I made it a novel to get here."

"Here, meaning drunk?"

"Yeah, and it's a fuckin' good thing." He took another swig.

Roddy flopped back into the blankets Gabe had thrown under him. If there was a sky above him, he couldn't see it for all the city lights. He wished for the heavenly lights of a campground, one that didn't catch fire. Actually, he felt pretty good as the booze took effect and his head spun. He seemed to be daydreaming in rapid succession from Jason, to Darrell, to Gabe and Shithead under the overpass, of the memorial service for the homeless that had died, to the time he struck his mother in the eye. He paused there for just a moment, then skidded away to Angela lying beside him in the park. Then Dad. Oh, shit, Dad, his dad would be furious. He couldn't stay here. He tried to rise, but stumbled onto Gabe who by now was singing some old folk song about loving someone who didn't love you, then broke into laughter as he pushed Roddy off him. "You ain't goin' anywhere tonight, man. You can't even walk."

"Oh shit, oh shit. Why'd I come here."

"You wanted to see me, remember?" Remember?" He grabbed Roddy's face between his hands and pushed his lips out as if to kiss him, then pushed him away. "God, you're pathetic, kid, really pathetic. You got the whole world lovin you, and you go burn down an old building and don't even get caught."

"I burned down two garages, too."

"You what? Shit man, you're an arsonist. God damn. And all I did was fuck the girl I loved. If she had been eighteen. . . . . What difference did it make? I loved her and she loved me. Where's the justice? And what the hell is goin' on with you?"

"I don't know. You're the only one I've told about this stuff."

"Why me?"

"Does it matter?"

"No, I suppose not. Go to sleep."

Roddy guessed that was the only option. He wasn't going anywhere and the Black Velvet had taken its toll. He fell asleep along the river whose swirling waters could transport his dreams to another life. But no dreams swirled with the waters. His brain was a *tabula rasa*, waiting for something new to be written and only he could be the author. Sometime toward morning before the first hint of light, he felt his stomach roiling, ready to evacuate its untenable contents. Soon he was crawling across the blankets in the near freezing night to a spot of bare ground amenable to what he had to offer. It wasn't pleasant, nor aromatic, but seemed almost like an epiphany, certainly a relief that left him sitting beside his profligacy in dizzy contemplation. What the hell was he doing? He pulled a blanket around his shoulders and tried to make sense out his behavior and especially out of what had to come next. But before he could dwell on the consequences with his parents, he realized that he had learned something in spite of his confused brain. Gabe had shown him what he didn't want to become. Gabe had created himself. Darrell had been a victim of injustices beyond his ability to transcend. So had Jason, but he could still survive. His life wasn't over. And Pete was gone, just plain gone. His dad was surviving. What about Emma and Angela? He, Roddy, should help. Whatever injustices and distresses Roddy experienced were minor compared to others. Look at Marty, for God sakes, a winner, scared to death of Trump, but rising above his circumstances.

Back under the blankets for a moment of warmth, he heard Gabe snore like the revving of a Harley Davidson, apparently content with his world, expecting nothing that hadn't already happened. It was time to go, no need to wake Gabe, no need to tell him goodbye. Roddy wasn't ever there for him, not yesterday or the day before or ever, and wouldn't be again. There was no

Gabe, just a guy who, by his own admission, lives in an ashcan, waiting for whomever to pass the time. Today it was Roddy. Now to get home, deal with reality of Dad and Mom and Julia. God, he had forgotten about Julia. He hoped she was all right. God it was cold, and dark. Maybe he could get home before his father knew he was gone. Fat chance. Even with the freedom his father had given him, he was ever aware now of where his son might be or not be. He was getting better at that. Roddy knew he had no means of escape. He would have to face the consequences.

He unlocked his bike from under the clump of trees where he had left it and rode westward. A mile or so up the road he saw a single light coming toward him on the bike path bigger than a bike light, a warning to his befuddled brain that something was awry. He twisted off the road falling into high grass and dragged himself and his bike behind a bush. The light was attached to a soft hum, a motorcycle but not a Harley, a Honda Goldwing, perhaps, with police officer glued to it. The light spotted the area including the bush that protected Roddy from view then continued on to the east. They were looking for him. He had no doubt about it. His dad had called the police, he hoped out of concern rather than anger, most likely both. Oh shit. Oh, shit. Suddenly he remembered his mobile phone in his backpack. He should call, plead guilty and beg him to call off the posse. He would be home soon. He was all right, just confused and disobedient and he was sorry. His mother was there, too, and Julia waiting for some word, hoping I was okay. His mom was crying, his dad trying to comfort her and Roger. Roger, too? Oh, my God. It was like he had hit his mother all over again. Maybe he had no future, maybe he was a Gabe. He had to face them, let them know how sorry he was, make no excuses. How could he explain? What if the police were there and asked questions, about Gabe. He couldn't tell them about Gabe. Gabe could get in real trouble for getting a minor drunk and whatever else. He would have to lie. He hated to lie but again found himself in a place where a lie was better than the truth or maybe the real truth, the real justice lay in the heart. Such gibberish to assure himself that he was basically an honest person, that his heart was sound. He hoped that somehow.

There was no police car in front of the house, not yet, but they would arrive in spite of his dad's call that his son had been found. He would have to explain. "I'm so sorry," he gushed to his mom's waiting arms, then Julia and his dad's "We were so worried." And Roger studying him as if he knew they would never get the whole story. Roddy sputtered and stuttered as the knock on the door stood between him and the truth. What truth? Roddy said to the awaiting circle, Mom, Dad, Julia, Roger and two officers. "I was upset. I just started riding into town where I had been before, to the homeless shelter where I had met Darrell. He died in the snow last December, you know. I didn't find him or anyone I knew but a couple of guys under the 94 bridge. They were drinking and they gave me a swig, or two. I couldn't ride home and fell asleep."

"We looked for you all over," the police woman said. "There wasn't anyone under the overpass,"

"I think that's where it was. I'm not sure now."

"Didn't you freeze?" Julia's question.

"They had blankets and newspapers. It wasn't so bad. I'm so sorry."

"Did you get their names?" The other officer inquired.

"No, I didn't ask." Roddy had said his piece and was satisfied he had told enough of the truth. What they needed to know was that he had been drinking and was safe. That was enough.

"We're glad you're safe," Policewoman said and rose to leave.

That's it. He was off the legal hook? No more grilling?

"You gave us such a scare," his mother said again. His dad nodded apparently not knowing what to say. Maybe he wouldn't yell at him. Maybe he would listen if Roddy talked. Maybe things were changing. Maybe both his dad and he were making some adjustments.

Collecting himself his dad suggested, "I think you need to get out of those clothes. They smell. You must have been sick."

"Yeah, I guess I was," Roddy responded sheepishly. "I'll go clean up. Thank you for understanding." He nodded to each.

He couldn't remember ever saying that before, even to Julia whom he definitely loved, but he said it. He said it. Astounding. His parents were understanding. He took a shower then climbed into bed in the early morning light amazed at what a drunken night could inspire. God his head hurt.

Light broke in through the window shades and pressed on his eyelids. Roddy's thoughts bounced like a released bag of ping ping balls. Pulling the pillow over his head, he tried to make sense of the previous night. He had confessed his sins to a man, a drunk man, not a priest, but almost like a priest in a confession booth, even though Roddy wasn't Catholic and had only heard about confessions and penance, but almost like a priest isolated in a grove of willow trees in the dark with a man who would have no interest in telling on him, who he himself had a crime to confess in the eyes of the law but not in his own because he was in love with her and wanted to marry her, but he was forbidden, and what happened to her, Roddy wanted to know and hadn't thought to ask, because he was only thinking about his own distress and wanted release from his crimes and from the tragedies surrounding him. He wondered what ensued that made Gabe lose his life and not even go in search of it. The words of confession that Roddy had blurted out had brought some relief. His pouring out was a kind of catharsis, even though a drunken one. He wasn't a drunk, not a discard in an ashcan, but a man in search of his hidden self, not lost, just not knowing where he was going. As for Gabe, there was nothing to be done, not for him, Roddy, anyway. Gabe would have to find himself if and when he had the inclination. It was noon when Roddy left his bed for a new day.

CHAPTER TWENTY-TWO

HIS SEVENTEENTH BIRTHDAY was non-descript, just a few cards and money and a chocolate cake passed between his Mom's and Dad's places. Fifty dollars to spend on whatever. Marty convinced Roddy to participate in the graduation ceremony the first week of June even though he couldn't receive his diploma until after he completed an English and a Social Studies credit in summer school. Only two graduates separated Martinez and Mattson in the graduation parade of some 550 young people, so the two friends marched together, miles apart in scholarship and preparation, but side by side in spirit. Marty received recognition for his full ride scholarship to Hamlin University to the smiling faces of his parents and sister while Roddy's parents sat anxiously hoping that Roddy's participation wasn't a deception, a premature celebration of what would never be. Roddy, Julia, and his parents attended the graduation party at the Martinez's, then ended the evening quietly with parental words of encouragement to their son.

So it was back to school for Roddy and a second summer with Mr. Sanchez, the English teacher, whom Roddy liked. He could do his assignments. He didn't know what to expect from Mr. Sandvik, the social studies teacher whom he knew nothing about, but he'd muddle through.

Sanchez had inspired Roddy to write about his anger the year before in some organized, presentable fashion and intrigued him with readings in both fact and fiction. Now Sanchez in a joint effort with Mr. Sandvik developed a project during this political season to examine journalism. "Measuring the news" Sanchez called it. He wanted students to investigate what reporters were writing about the presidential candidates in quality and quantity and to extrapolate from their investigation the effects of their writings on the polls. For two weeks they would, with ruler and paper and pencil, examine the *Minneapolis Star and Tribune* and the *New York Times* for the number of inches in columns of news devoted to each of the candidates and to compare the results with polling statistics. Then they would determine how much was positive and how much negative and finally how much the candidates spoke to particular issues and how much to bluster. The reason for this project was clear. Especially among the Republican candidates there seemed to be more bluster than substance, more demeaning comments and personal attacks. The Democrats seemed to settle in on Hillary Clinton with a massive lead, but a climbing Bernie Sanders strived for attention. At onset, Roddy thought the study a bunch of busy work, but soon found the class discoveries interesting if not arresting.

To parallel the project, the teachers instructed the students to decipher the differences between fact and opinion and logical fallacies. A statement of fact could be true or false and provable, an opinion not provable and therefore not suitable for argument. "Low carb diets are healthier than low fat diets" is a statement of preference rather than proof and therefore is an opinion. "Chicago is a larger city than Minneapolis" is a statement of fact because it can be proven. A simple investigation would prove this fact statement to be true. However, "There are 3500 feet in a mile" is a statement of fact but is false because it can be proven to be 5280 feet. Often then statements of fact must be tested against available data and proofs. When Bill Clinton said, "I didn't have sex with that woman," he made a statement of fact, but evidence showed the contrary based on an accepted definition of sex and his behavior, so his statement of fact was false. Most politicians attempt to make true statements of fact, but often fail to have all the information necessary to support their statements. To say that some intentionally mislead constituents is an opinion impossible to prove. Before long Roddy and classmates were deeply involved and eager for the outcome.

In the meantime the campaigns of both parties headed into their nominating conventions throwing verbal punches right and left. From student research Donald Trump had received far more coverage, almost twice as much, as any other Republican candidate in spite of the polls showing that Ted Cruz was clearly in the lead and Ben Carson following some distance behind. In the Democratic race, Hillary Clinton was receiving far more coverage than Bernie Sanders in spite his escalating poll numbers. The question then became, To what degree did the amount of coverage, positive and negative, affect the nomination process and would it be equally significant in determining the outcome of the election in November?

On one of Roddy's many visits to Jason and his usual inquiry about how Jason's mom and sister were coping after the loss of Pete and Jason's expected answer, "as well as can be expected," Roddy brought his interest in his school project to Jason's attention while the two of them exercised on the Maxim gym equipment Jason's mom had provided in the den. Although Roddy had taken only a mild interest in the election at the time of their Trump rally visit in Eau Claire, his summer school course work had led him to study the candidates more closely. As they did their reps, he probed Jason for his current take on Trump to discover that he was vacillating somewhat from his former enthusiasm. Recently Trump had made fun of a disabled reporter with what appeared to be a paralyzed hand gesture to which his supporters laughed, his point being that the reporter was incompetent. Jason saw himself as the butt of the joke. It reminded him, too, of Trump's comment that McCain was no hero because he was captured. He mentioned both of these crudités to Roddy as they relaxed on the floor mat for their stretching exercises. Roddy, probing deeper, commented on Trump's diatribe about Mexicans being rapists and criminals and that we needed to build a wall to keep them out. Jason's defensive reply was, "We let them come in here and take our jobs and threaten our way of life. It won't be long before their drug gangs will take over and we'll have to wall ourselves in to protect ourselves."

"Why do you think they want to come here, Jason? Huh? Isn't it because they want a better life for their families just as our ancestors did?"

"Maybe, but why can't they apply legally so we can make sure they aren't criminals?"

"Well, yeah, we have to have better regulations, but do you think a wall is the answer?"

"It would help."

"You've met my friend Marty. He's Guatemalan. He came here with his family because his father was threatened by gang members. He wanted safety and a better life with a good job. He's smart and Marty is a straight A student and going to Hamlin University. He's one Latino that isn't a criminal. You can't blame all Mexicans or Guatemalans or any ethnic or racial group because of a few bad apples."

"Yeah, I know, but Trump is a business man who swears he can create jobs for people and make other NATO countries pay their fair share for defense, and get rid of Obamacare and replace it with the best healthcare system we've ever seen. I believe he can do it."

"I wish he could, but pay attention to what he says. Does he really have a plan?"

"I think he does. He just isn't laying his cards on the table for his opponents to tear up before he gets a chance to win the bet. "

"Maybe."

That ended the conversation. Roddy realized that his argument had clarified his own thinking. They hadn't even mentioned Trump's demeaning of women in the past and more recently with his crude comment about news commentator Megan Kelly. That was repulsive. That was no way to talk. He thought about his sister and Angela. They shouldn't have to hear a candidate for the highest office in the land demean their gender. Enough for now. He had other things to think about, Angela, for one. How was she coping? She was going to school. He hadn't seen her since the funeral too many days ago. She was never home when Roddy came to visit. He had her phone number. He could call her, but should he? Was she ready to talk with him? He'd wait a bit longer. Then he called her.

"Are you okay? It's Roddy."

"I know. I'm all right," she responded without conviction.

"May I come over?"

"I have a lot of school work to do, but. . . Sure come over. It will be good to see you."

Roddy shuddered. So much had happened since their "date," almost too long ago to know where to start a conversation. But he had made a commitment. He wanted her to know how sorry he was about their loss, hers, her mother's and Jason's, and his, too, because he respected Pete a lot. He was a good father, for sure, and Roddy assumed he was a good husband. He had no reason to think otherwise. He would let Angela talk about whatever mattered to her. He wouldn't have to say much at all, just be supportive, mind his manners, and not pretend to know how she felt, and not be patronizing, whatever that meant, but he'd know if it happened and she felt minimized. He wanted her to feel comfortable with him as she had before and he had with her in spite of the changes that had taken place in both of their lives.

He brought her flowers, jonquils and irises, to accompany his words of condolences for her loss. That she hadn't expected. She teared up, then turned away, supposedly to find a vase but mostly to hide her emotions. "That's very thoughtful of you, Roddy," she smiled when she returned and motioned for him to sit across from her in the den, the all purpose room, beside the Maxim gym. Jason was in his room. Emma was in the kitchen preparing a strawberry pie ala mode. When she presented her culinary gift, Roddy was surprised to see his father entering behind her from the kitchen. "Dad!" He nearly shouted.

"Yes, hi, son. I was helping Emma with some plumbing issues. The kitchen sink needs a good reaming. I'll take care of it in the morning. I need to get home. See you tomorrow, Emma. See you later, Roddy." He smiled at each then took his leave.

Roddy remained startled knowing full well there was more to this visit than the kitchen sink, but how could there be? The Johnsons and Mattsons had been close friends for a long time, but was there more to it than that or was his dad just being neighborly? He let it go. He was here to see Angela and she seemed to have no such curiosity.

Roddy asked her about school. What she enjoyed most was her poetry class as he suspected, but she didn't offer him another poem at the moment. Instead she talked about how poets helped her to feel deeply and understand on a more universal level the human experience. They helped her cope with her father's untimely death. As she spoke she smiled at him as if to say everything was all right and meant it, that somehow her father's death was an acceptable event in the planet's affairs. What did she mean? She wasn't angry? She let him go? Roddy was confused. Yes, of course, they couldn't bring him back. There was no use in dwelling on his passing forever, but how could she and Emma, too, let him go so soon? How does one suffer and move on? How does one rue one's past and move forward in full realization of one's failures. What did that have to do with her loss? Or was it in both cases a loss of innocence? An innocence that never really ever disappears in spite of many experiences. What Roddy realized more than ever was that Angela was beautiful sitting there smiling, teaching, caressing him with her words. She really liked him. Roddy could feel it. He was amazed and oh so thankful. And he smiled, too. Emma encouraged them to eat the dessert.

CHAPTER TWENTY-THREE

RODDY SURVIVED SUMMER school with better than passing grades. He might have excelled had his reading and writing skills been more developed. Most important he had learned that he wanted to learn. He had become fascinated with the "war of the media" as Mr. Sanchez called it, i.e. the marketing ploys that the several media used to win customers. Most of them apparently were negative. The more scandalous the better. He wanted more than ever to be able to discern truth from fantasy or false statements. What Sanchez had taught them in his six week course was pertinent to the outside world. His lessons addressed the controversies among concerned citizens trying to decipher the integrity of each candidate for public office. Within two weeks Roddy received his diploma in the mail. He was a high school graduate. Yeah, but without a future. Marty was heading to college, Angela was in college now. Who was he if not dead end, Roddy? But he didn't say so, even if he thought it, not to anyone.

It wasn't Gabe, certainly, but it was downtown, the downtown of Darrell, the underbelly of dissent and penury, dressed in the glass and steel of prosperity. It was the underbelly that he felt part of, the holy grail of his redemption where he had confessed once in the dark to one who had no authority to forgive, only to acknowledge his crime, even shame him for it as he had shamed himself but unable to bring his shame to light. Downtown, alone, by bike, the transportation of his former self replaced by the illusion of adulthood in his sluggish VW. That automobile had to be fixed. Both he and it needed a valve job. Roger could arrange for that and would when he had the money or thought it worth his while. For now, however, it was downtown by bike.

    Roddy had paid attention to the news. On July 7, the same week he finished summer school and earned his diploma, a policeman pulled over Philander Castile driving with his girlfriend and 4 year old daughter in Falcon Heights when Castile apparently reached for his driver's license and was shot dead as his girlfriend taped the incident on her mobile phone video. This happened the day after a police shooting of a black man in Louisiana. On Saturday, the 9th, protesters gathered across I94 to shut down traffic and demand justice for this needless shooting. Now on Sunday afternoon Roddy learned that a few hundred people were marching in protest on Hennepin and 9th Ave. This was a bikeable event to his downtown, his underbelly downtown, where paraders were calling for justice. He rode in, locked his bike to a light post by the bus station and walked to Hennepin. Many protesters were carrying signs "Black Lives Matter." "Peace and Love" "No more shootings." Roddy found himself following the crowd down Hennepin and west to the Target Center, where speakers on P.A decried the brutality and criminal assault on black people. Roddy felt like one of them, alone, angry, not for himself anymore but more at himself for not taking advantage of opportunities, for letting his anger guide his behavior rather than justice. Now he could focus his anger toward what mattered. These people were speaking the truth. Black lives did matter but the criminal justice system didn't

The Stranger Who Was Himself

operate accordingly. Blacks were easily discarded. So were the homeless, so were disabled veterans. So he marched.

Suddenly from the bystanders a man threw a bottle into the paraders and struck a black woman who was carrying a child. As she sunk to the pavement, Roddy sprinted after the culprit, caught up with him in a tackle and pounded him in the face with his right fist. Before he could strike again he felt his left side explode in pain, then his head whirl with a blow that sent his eyes spinning and blue light blind him. A police woman shined a light back and forth across his blurred vision. "Are you all right?" She inquired.

"I think so." He blinked a few times until he saw her face.

"Here, I'll help you up."

Roddy struggled to his feet overcoming the pain in his side and tried to appraise his situation.

"I saw what happened. The woman who was hit will be all right." She waited for Roddy to digest what she had said. "We caught the bottle thrower."

Roddy nodded without words.

"You could have started a riot. I could arrest you for assault. You broke his nose."

Roddy was alert now and realized he was on the edge. Whatever he said could go against him, but he had to give it a try.

"I'm sorry I should have helped the woman instead of attacking that idiot. I shouldn't have hit him."

"No question he deserved it, but you can't beat up people, not even those who deserve it."

"I know. I'm sorry." He wasn't sorry for the guy he hit but sorry that he let his anger get the best of him.

"Where do you live?"

"In Hopkins."

"Do you have transportation?
"My bike."
"Can you ride?"
"Yeah, I'm okay."
"Go home. This isn't your problem."

She was letting him go. Isn't his problem? What did she mean? He wasn't suppose to be protesting injustice? Did she think a trigger happy cop was just a black man's problem? That's the problem. He peddled home favoring his right side from the blow someone had struck him. His downtown, his other world, receding behind him.

No one was home when he arrived. He found a note from his dad on the kitchen table that said that he and Julia had gone to the Y for exercise and a swim. Fine. He'd have time to assess his bodily damage without inquiry. Nothing showed except the lump on his head covered with hair. He was glad he hadn't gotten the haircut he needed. His right side hurt but didn't show signs of abuse. That might change in a day or two, but it appeared there would be no need for inquiry and their wasn't. The news that evening carried no account of the incident, so the brief skirmish had not been recorded. In fact, the march was said to be a quiet protest without undue disruption and arrests. Roddy congratulated himself on his participation, but grimaced at the thought of his violent outburst, then smiled to the realization that he had broken the bottle thrower's nose. You can't be sorry and gratified at the same time, he thought, but he was, which meant that he hadn't fully come to terms with his intemperate behavior, his impulsive outbursts that could one day cause him to change the course of his life and maybe the life of another.

CHAPTER TWENTY-FOUR

HIS PARENTS THREW A PARTY, the one he should have had in June when the real students graduated, instead of August. Angela came and Jason who was still waiting for a prosthesis, but was quite ambulatory on crutches. It was amazing how he could swing his body around, up stairs and down, almost in a run, preferring the sticks, as he called them, to the wheelchair. His trousers were cut so that the empty leg fit snuggly against his hip and appeared to be his special fashion. And he was spirited with a positive pissed off demeanor that wasn't offensive as much as enticing. What he was pissed off about had taken a u turn at the political intersection of civility and boorishness. Trump was a boor, a disgusting liar that had no respect for those who cared most about their country, like him, like McCain, like thousands of men and women who had fought for freedom, many of whom, like him, had paid a high price for their commitment and no respect for women like his beautiful mother and sister who needed financial support to reach their potential without the help of a husband and father. Angela wanted to be a teacher and that demanded a costly education. Scholarships weren't enough. She needed government loans at a low interest rate, so that she wouldn't be in debt for the rest of her life. Damn, he was angry at all of the candidates. They had more interest in getting elected than in serving the people once they obtained office. To hell with them all.

"What about Bernie Sanders?" Roddy posited.

"Who listens to a goddamn socialist. That's not the American way."

"If the American way is to pull yourself up by your own bootstraps, you better have boots. So what do you want, Jason?"

"I want a government that cares about its people, like you, me, Angela, Mom, and your dad who is trying to compete in the hardware business with Walmart and Home Depot and Menards."

"So do I. That's why I've listened to Marty, who wants a government who respects the millions of immigrants who have come here from all over the world for three centuries to earn a better life for themselves. Marty, an American citizen, was born to illegal immigrants who are still illegal because this government under the leadership of Republicans or Democrats hasn't been able to come up with a reasonable, timely plan to citizenship and the leading Republican candidate calls Mexicans, by which he means all Latinos, rapists and scum. So I go with Marty. I'm for the Burn."

"When did you decide that?"

"Just now as I listened to the two of us talk. I've been studying all the political games the media make out of it and I'm ready to join the only candidate that appeals directly to the people with an agenda that matters to us. And he won't take any of the corporate money that buys the candidate's allegiance. He's his own man."

"Trump is his own man, too, but he's an asshole."

"So we agree."

"I don't know. Maybe an asshole is better than a Socialist."

"You think?"

They left the question hanging in the air. Jason realized he had upended his allegiance in a fit of pique and come up short. He still thought Trump had the makings of a President who could assault the stalemate of two parties so entrenched and so beholden to special interests that he could succeed. But he had to admit that Trump pissed him off with his profligate tweets. How hard would it be for him to hold his tongue? Too hard, apparently. Still he thought him the best of the Republican candidates to get the nomination. Ted Cruz, God no. Such a phony. And Jeb Bush? Nice guy, but no personality and no confrontational powers. Carson? How did he ever become a neurological surgeon? He can't even talk. So it's Trump in spite of his mouth, and his women. After all Bill Clinton was no saint, but did some good things for the economy except that he bought into the big bucks and his wife followed suit. Shit, what a mess.

To which Roddy said, "Shit, what a mess." What was he, Roddy, so impassioned about? He couldn't vote. Let it be. His day would come. Then again, he didn't have to vote to make a difference. He could work with Marty. Is that what he wanted to do? And what about his family? His father, for example. Where was he on these candidates? Did it matter? Last time he mentioned it his dad had indicated a preference for Hillary. Was that simply because he had always voted Democrat or because he had the conviction that she would make a good President? And why Sanders over Clinton? Could he win? Or was his dad right that Clinton could beat any of the Republicans vying for nomination? What the hell was he getting so worked up about? This was not his war, not yet. He was more interested in what he was going to do next after having a diploma but no destiny.

He wished he could talk with his dad or his mom for that matter. But she always said to follow his heart and that he was very smart and could do whatever he wanted to. Very encouraging, but not convincing. His dad, on the other hand, encouraged him to continue his education now that he could see that Roddy had caught a bit of fire from Mr. Sanchez. He advised him to go to Hennepin or Normandale Jr. College for preparation until he discovered what he wanted to do. He knew what he wanted to do. He wanted to be an investigative journalist, discover the truth from all the prevarications the American public had to sort through in every speech from a candidate. He wanted to expose hypocrisy fully aware of his own falsity. He didn't tell lies. He only hid the truth. And he hadn't squelched the fire inside. So he and Marty and Juanita worked for Sanders, putting up lawn signs, door knocking, convinced after the early polls showing Sander's Minnesota lead that he could win the nomination only to despair at the Democratic National Committee bias that, with the help of the committed superdelegates swept Hillary Clinton into the nomination. Sanders would declare his support for her in spite of his protest that the nomination was fixed. Trump had won his parties nomination and certainly Clinton needed everyone's support to beat him. Roddy despaired, however. He hated Sander's capitulation as much as Marty did. He had convinced himself that Sanders was the savior to the American system. But it wasn't to be. So now what? Let it pass. Let the winds blow as they may. He needed a break.

CHAPTER TWENTY-FIVE

PER ROGER'S FACILITATION Roddy drove his reluctant VW to the GO-A-Ginn Autoworks off Central Avenue in Northeast Minneapolis for a compression check that would proved he needed an engine overhaul, at least a valve grinding and new rings. The owner-proprietor and chief mechanic greeted him with "So you're going to be Roger's stepson."

"Ya, I guess."

"I'm Lawrence Little Bear. Call me Larry. Glad to meet you."

"I'm Roddy. He said we could make a deal on repair."

"Probably." The two eyed each other with interest.

"Are you an Indian?"

Little Bear laughed and sounded a war whoop, "Wooo Wooo Woop, Aieeeee."

"Sorry, I didn't mean it that way."

"What way did you mean it? Don't you think Indians are real? I'm real and I'm a Native American and you and I will be friends once you learn a few things."

Roddy realized he was about to "learn a few things" and he was ready. He thought Native Americans were on reservations or drunks that lived off Cedar Avenue.

"You own this place?"

"Amazing isn't it?"

"Ya, I guess."

"So you don't have to guess anymore, I'm from the Standing Rock reservation, a Hunkpapa Dakota of the Lakota clan. I worked as a mechanic for ten years before I had enough money to buy this place with the help of some friends and no help from a bank. I'm good. I don't drink. I send money back to my family. My youngest sister "completed" as we say, ie, she committed suicide, so did my cousin. My father was killed in a knife fight fifteen years ago and my mother's a drunk. Let's get to work."

"Wait, what's it going to cost me?"

"Your education."

"Huh?"

"Have you been watching the news?"

"You mean about the campaign?"

"Yes, of course, and about the Pipeline, the Dakota Access Pipeline DAPL."

"No, I guess I haven't."

"There you go guessing again."

"The oil companies have permission from the Army Corp of Engineers to run a oil pipeline through our reservation, under the Missouri River, our source of water, through South Dakota all the way to Illinois where the oil will be transported to Texas for refining. That's our land, our water and they endanger it. We've already had one oil spill from the Keystone Pipeline of some million gallons that endangered species and polluted our water, but they assure us that no such thing will happen again with this new pipeline. Right. Our young people have formed an alliance to protest near Cannon Ball, North Dakota. They have marched to Omaha to protest the Army Corp decision and continued on to Washington DC when that protest failed. Native youth are gathering by the hundreds, maybe thousands along the Missouri River in peaceful protest and prayer. And I'm going to join them soon."

"What will you do there?"

"Pray, sing, carry signs, block roadways, stop rubber bullets, breathe tear gas, turn the other cheek."

Roddy stared at him transfixed.

"What do you expect will happen?"

"We'll stop the political and corporate machine from destroying our land and polluting our water. We'll bring the fractured Sioux Nation together and give them a reason to be living, a future to hope for after the dismal treatment we have received through broken treaties and divided lands. We're coming together now for all people, not just native people, for all people and the earth, our mother that corporations are gutting and bleeding. Our youth are leading even our elders who have almost given up in despair. Our youth won't let them and as old as I am, I'm with them."

Roddy felt the burning inside. This man was amazing. How did Roger know him? Why did he bring the two of them together?

"Roger says you don't know what to do with yourself. You graduated from high school, right?"

"Yes."

"You're not going to college."

"Not yet."

"You need something to do."

"Maybe." Roddy studied him wearily.

"Let's tear this VW down."

"You want me to help?"

"You got anything better to do?"

"No, I guess not."

"You're a guessing little bastard, aren't ya."

Roddy almost said it again but caught himself.

"Drive into stall #1 and pop the hood."

Roddy did as directed. Larry in apron and safety goggles started the task of disconnecting the battery, draining fluids, removing wires, and vacuum hoses and wires around intake manifold, instructing Roddy from time to time to hand him implements like a surgeon's assistant. Before long the two of them had removed the intake manifold, exhaust system, and head gasket. They were ready for the valve job. Roddy, too, in goggles and apron, assisted as directed and watched in admiration, observing Larry's every move, still not knowing what the cost of this procedure would be. They had been working for two hours when Larry addressed him.

"So how much do you think you can pay?"

"Not much."

"I didn't think so. It'll cost you what you're worth."

"What does that mean?"

"It means that you have to learn some things about engines and do what I tell you. It means that you need to learn some things about what matters."

Roddy was speechless. Larry was offering to teach him. He didn't know what he was more interested in, mechanics or his life. Maybe it was both that somehow became the mechanics of life. "So what has kept you busy since you graduated?"

"I was working on the Bernie Sanders campaign until Clinton was endorsed. I'll vote for her but I lost my enthusiasm for politics. My friend Marty convinced me that Trump is a disaster. I'm not committed to anything right now."

"See ya tomorrow."

"We're done already?"

"it's 3 o'clock. I have things to do." Larry led Roddy out the door and locked it.

"What time?"

"About one. I'm at the American Indian Center all morning." He opened his passenger car door, an older Subaru Legacy. "Hop in. I'll give ya a ride home."

"Oh, ya, it's a ways to walk."

He drove Roddy to his mom's house. Roddy plopped into his favorite green swivel chair, tilted back and closed his eyes. He had nothing to do and nowhere to go. His bike was at his dad's. He wasn't tired but fell asleep. Roadways passed before him, long stretches of pavement toward hills, through towns, people along side calling to him, people holding signs he couldn't read, deer crossing in front of him in herds, engine parts lying along side, buildings burning, a man on a platform hooking up a banner to the sky without words or images, no end, just roads going on and on, empty roads with people waving as he passed and then there was Angela just ahead within a few feet ahead smiling. She turned and motioned for him to follow to the river crossing the road.

"Did you see Larry?" Roger stood over him as he tried to make out where he was.

"Yeah, we worked on my car, didn't say what it would cost me, interesting guy."

"He's interesting, all right."

"How do you know him.?"

"We became friends at Patrick Henry High. He taught me a few things."

"Like what?"

"How to fix cars for one thing. That's why I became a systems analyst."

"But that's not all."

"No, that's not all." He paused as he snuggled into the matching green swivel across from Roddy. "He connected me to the earth."

Roddy studied his mother's boyfriend and waited for more.

"I spent time with him on the reservation. He told me about the ghost dances of his ancestors. I sat with him in council tipi and passed the pipe around the circle of men and watched the smoke ascend through the smoke hole and heard the leader chant. I felt like one of them but knew I wasn't and couldn't be but Larry made it possible for me to love your mother."

This wasn't making any sense. His insides were roiling. It wasn't the burning now, no fire, that had seared his insides so many times, but a whirling, a twisting, a churning that made him want to run. Roddy struggled from the chair, poured a glass of milk from the fridge and returned to the green chair.

The churning subsided to a feathery touch. He liked it. He wanted to learn more.

"Larry will teach you." Roger rose, went to the kitchen and uncapped a Blue Moon. He had said enough apparently.

"Thanks, Roger."

"Your welcome." He disappeared to the back porch and left Roddy to think about his unusual afternoon.

"How'd you meet Roger, Mom?" Roddy blurted as his mother fussed with the food she was preparing for dinner.

"A man I met at the bookstore introduced me to him. His name is Larry Little Bear. He came into the bookstore to read Louise Erdrich books. Never bought them, but that was okay. Sometimes he'd just closed his eyes, didn't sleep, just meditated, I think. We talked a lot he and I. Then one day he told me he wanted to introduce me to a man I might like. He knew I was single. I had told him about the divorce. So I said, fine, and I went with him after work to Roger's auto shop. Roger was expecting me. I liked him right away. That's how it started. Why do you ask?"

"Larry is overhauling my VW and I'm helping him. It was not something Roger could do. He hasn't told me what it will cost me. I'm a little nervous about it."

"Don't be. It'll be fine."

"How come I haven't met him before?"

"I don't know, just hasn't happened."

"He says he's going to Standing Rock pretty soon. Do you know what's going on there?"

"Yes, it's terrible."

"I think I want to go with him." Roddy didn't know he was going to say that, but as he said it he felt that feathery touch.

"Really? You would do that? I'd worry about you. It could be dangerous."

This wasn't the mother he thought she was. She had changed. She didn't say, no, just that she'd worry about him, not that she could stop him from going, but that she had a life he didn't know about from the bookstore and Larry Little Bear and then Roger. She was different from his mother who had fought so with his dad.

"I want to go with you," Roddy said as they unbolted the valves from the VW the next afternoon. "We'll take my car when we're done. I watched the news last night. I want to protest that pipeline. I can make signs. I'm good at it. I used to paint a lot."

"Of course. You pay for the gas. That's your cost for the valve job."

Roddy couldn't wait to tell Marty. It seemed Larry had known Roddy would go with him from the start. Maybe Roger did, too. He was feathery inside as if a pillow had exploded, the dream road was winding toward a destination he couldn't see but knew was the right direction, such confused images, so much excitement, so much faith. Marty wished he could go, too, but he had to start Hamlin University. But he'd go in spirit. That's what it was. Spirit. That's what the feathers were about, Hope. Angela had read him something like that.

Sunday afternoon Roger took him to his dad's where he hopped on his bike and rode to see Angela and Jason. They were both at home. And Emma, too. He jabbered so fast they could hardly follow his words. So he had met Larry Little Bear who was fixing his car and with whom he was going to Standing Rock Reservation to protest the pipeline. Emma was aghast. Jason, skeptical, and Angela beaming. He said Marty couldn't go, because he was in college, but he, Roddy, was going and he felt the feathers tickling him all over.

He had to talk to Angela alone. He would discuss the matter with Jason later. But it was Angela he needed to talk to. He believed she would support him. He didn't expect her to go with him. This was to be just Roddy and Larry, who it seemed Roddy had known for a long time, not just a few days. Roddy and Angela sat in the empty bakery over a cup of coffee and muffin as they had so often and talked. She gave him her blessing and wished she had the right poem for him. She would find it and kissed him on the cheek.

CHAPTER TWENTY-SIX

MUCH HAD TO BE DONE in preparation for the journey. Besides the approval of Mom and Dad, which at first was reluctant then acquiescent, the two adventurers, soon to be demonstrators or protesters, or both, had to finish VW repair. That they did in the following week. Also they needed to bring supplies —water and food, sleeping bags, tents, propane heaters for the chilly September and maybe October nights. Roddy packed paints and poster board for making signs. They had no idea how long they would stay. They might become suppliers traveling from town to town, church to church, to pick up supplies collected through GoFundMe and other solicitations. Or they might help to build temporary housing for the many supporters arriving from the nearby reservations Rosebud and Cheyenne, even further away, from Apache and Navajo in Arizona.

The American Indian Center on Franklin Avenue was rapidly becoming a warehouse for supplies and Roddy and Larry could transport as much as they could pack into the backseat and trunk of the Blue Beetle along with the personal belongings they would need for their stay. Rumors circulated that the North Dakota governor had established a $1000 fine for those bringing in supplies, but that the edict was hardly enforced. Nevertheless, it was clear that any attempt by the protesters to disrupt the construction process would meet with resistance.

With the car packed to the brim the two fellows started up I94 toward Fargo where they rested for the night with Larry's friend who warned them they would meet with resistance at the blockaded entrance. Their best entry, Jonah said, would be via Bismarck, south through Mandan, then on highway 6 south to the west of Cannon Ball, then east to the protesters Oceti Sakowin camp. That they did. When they arrived they drove through the encampment among the tipis and tents and sanitary stations until they found a parking area. Men and women in Indian attire and headdresses gathered around with happy greetings at the sight of supplies and more supporters. They set up the three man tent that still smelled smokey from its near fatal outing in Southeastern Minnesota, rolled out their sleeping bags and unzipped their suitcases. TO They sat up the three man tent that Roddy had purchased to replace the one lost in near fatal fire in Southwestern Minnesota, then rolled out their sleeping bags and unzipped their suitcases. On top of his clothes a note read, "Look under the floor mat of the driver's side of your car." Too curious to wait, he did so. He found an envelop with the note, "Take care of yourself, love Dad" and inside $300 in twenties. No strings attached. Roddy had some rethinking to do. Was his dad supporting him in his cause or simply providing some insurance just in case? In either case the money was welcome and his dad was thoughtful. He wished he could call him immediately and thank him but discovered there was no phone service in the camp.

It soon became apparent that these native people were committed to a mission and were gathering in sacred expression of their cause. They moved together like birds or rather like a herd of buffalo upon sacred ground fed by sacred water. In fact, buffalo did roam nearby. The new comers set up camp on sacred burial land that would soon be plowed up to receive a pipeline that would carry dirty, fracked oil from the Bakker fields near Williston to Indiana. Amid legal contention, the Dakota Access Pipeline crawled southward like a black snake to cross under the Missouri River and endanger the water supply of the native people. These people were standing for their rights, the rights to the land and water guaranteed by the Laramie Treaty of 1851. Their youth had marched to Omaha to protest to the Army Corp of Engineers and then to Washington DC. Obama had halted the pipeline progress for an environmental impact study, but the protesters were not going to abandoned their three camps. Amy Goodman from *Democracy Now* arrived to film and report the happenings. She caught on film the excessive use of force, shots of rubber bullets and water cannons spraying people who flocked to the Cannon Ball River to avoid the onslaught and to escape the slashing teeth of police dogs. Demonstrators watched as Goodman was taken into custody and prevented from showing her footage. Now she demanded freedom of the press as a constitutional right to tell what she saw.

Roddy made signs. PROTECT OUR WATER; NO DAPL; WATER IS LIFE; RESPECT OUR RIGHTS; THIS IS OUR LAND. At night he and Larry sat with native youth and listened as they chanted their peace songs. Then the meditative silence, the sense of being there in that place, now, projecting outward away from themselves into future generations who depended on them to preserve their land and water. They were prayerful, peaceful, determined to stand in the face of assault from the corporate machinery that bulldozed their future. There was Jasilyn Charger, a Lakota from the Cheyenne Reservation and a survivor of a suicide attempt, who had returned from Oregon, to become a leader of the movement, and Eryn Wise, a Jicarilla Apache from the Laguna Pueblo, who came from Minneapolis to represent Honor the Earth and provide inspiration for this vital cause.

Roddy, although not one of them, felt like one of them. Never had he felt more necessary than he did in this camp, providing supplies, making signs, standing before snarling dogs. He was afraid but never more at peace. He thought of Larry's story and the many suicides of these depressed people who had been discarded for decades by the manifest destiny of the pioneer movement, of the broken treaties, of the forced enculturation in white schools that stripped them of their traditions and sacred rites, even their language, and forced them to be farmers on land useful only for hunting, then splitting them into several reservations that left them fractured and useless. Now the native youth saw another kind of last stand, once more for their lives, for their way of life, for hope and the future of their people and Roddy felt that hope. He embraced it. He drank it in like the water of life that he needed to discover himself. These moments here at Standing Rock brought a calm sense of meaning that he vowed he would carry with him.

On the third day of his arrival one of the dogs broke loose and sunk its teeth into his left leg. It tore the flesh so that he had to be transported to Mandan for treatment. Amy Goodman photographed it, not his face, only his wound and the wounds of several others. The encampment had to move to make way for the machinery digging up their ground. But the people, now in the thousands from several reservations and other sympathetic supporters wouldn't budge until they were pelted with rubber bullets, tear gas and vicious dogs. Since the medical supplies and medic station was inadequate to tend to dog bites, medics applied antibiotics salves to the wound and bandaged it before transporting Roddy and David Finch, a social worker from Minneapolis, to Vibra Hospital in Mandan.

On the way David explained that he worked with many Native Americans via the American Indian Center near Cedar and Franklin Avenues in Minneapolis.

"Why did you decide to come here?" Roddy inquired.

"Because this cause is the most important effort for Native Americans in a hundred years. Theirs is a depressed culture that has had no way to sustain itself, fraught with alcoholism and suicide, broken relationships, truancy, poverty, meaninglessness. This movement to stop the pipeline is their hope for resurrection. It means they can be an integral part of saving their reservation and the earth from toxic waste that destroys the environment. This cause gives them hope. It gives them life." He paused. "And why are you here?"

Larry Little Bear repaired my Beetle and suggested I join him on this journey to pay for his work. He told me a bit of his story that confirmed what you just said. It seemed right to me to come and I'm glad I did."

"Even now, with a gash in your leg waiting for attention? You think you know why you have come?"

"I'm beginning to understand. Their energy and commitment are inspiring. They have purpose, something I'm searching for."

"So now what? Are you going back to camp after they sew you up?"

"I think so. I have some money to live on for a while. I feel that I matter here."

After filling out papers in the emergency room, each was ushered into a cubicle behind a curtain where an intern inquired about the incident.

"This was unwarranted hostility. I'll report it and make sure authorities understand this is abuse. Did you attack the police? Did you throw things at them?"

"No, we just stood our ground and they came at us."

"Not right. You'll need a tetanus inoculation but not rabies procedure. Police dogs are not infected. But I urge you to stay nearby for a couple of days and come in for a follow up to make sure the wound doesn't become infected."

Roddy received stitches, no charge from the sympathetic intern, and an order by a police sergeant not to return to Oceti Sakowin camp. The order seemed weak, however, unsubstantial, as if it came from a failed authority seeking to regain control of a hopeless situation. Roddy would return if he wanted to, the order notwithstanding. He felt powerful in peace. The fire inside him was no longer angry, but rather a passion for the right, not a burning as an expression of frustration and confusion but a flame of commitment. So what would he do? He would pick up more supplies, especially canned food like tuna, salmon, peas, beans, five gallon demijohns of drinking water, not water bottled in plastic. He was part of the Save the Earth revolution. He needed more signs. This wasn't just about Native American people. This was about the planet. No more oil. He wasn't ready to listen to the other side who asserted the needs for a transportation dependent on gasoline. There wasn't one. Nope, not this time.

Do you have a place to stay?" The intern asked.

"I can stay in a motel."

"No, go to the Unitarian Universalist church in Bismarck. It's only about ten miles east. They have showered the camps with food and supplies. Do you have a mobile phone?

"Yes, I'll call them."

Then Larry appeared from behind the curtain.

"How did you get here?" Roddy asked astounded.

"In your VW."

"What? I have the key."

"So I hot wired it."

"Why'd you come?

"Because we should head back to Minneapolis. My mother is sick. We might pack up another load and return later on, if you want to. I do."

"The intern wants me to stay a couple of days to be sure my wound is healing properly, but I suppose I can get it checked in Minneapolis."

Roddy didn't contact the UU church. He didn't return to Oceti Sakowin camp, not because of the police sergeant's demand, but because of Larry. He said goodbye to David Finch, and Larry and Roddy drove east, Larry driving. Roddy called his mom first with assurances that he was all right. She had seen the CNN the Amy Goodman footage of water cannons and snarling dogs and a shot of leg bites and then a disrupted camera shot as the photographer was pushed to the ground. Anderson Cooper announced that Goodman had been arrested and then released.

"Yes, Mom, that could be my leg. It's all patched up and I'm coming home. The people here are great. They want peace and safety and clean water, thousands of them. It's incredible."

Then he called his dad. At first he didn't know what to say except, "Thanks, Dad. I haven't spent any of the money. We had what we needed. Tell me, do you support the Native American's rights or do you just want me to have what I need?"

"Both. I'm proud of you, son."

Roddy didn't know what to say. He hadn't ever heard these words from his dad. The truth was he had never thought those words for himself. He had too much regret, too much baggage to carry around with him to truly be proud of himself. Maybe he had to confess his crimes. If so, to whom? Maybe his dad would understand now. Maybe Larry would. Yes, maybe he should confess to Larry and assess the outcome. Larry wouldn't tell on him. Why would he? He knew people were flawed. He knew many people who have gotten away with things.

They drove in silence for miles. Larry chanted peace songs that resonated throughout the vehicle and through Roddy's flesh like healing vibrations. Then silence until Roddy spoke.

"I have things to tell you if you will listen."

"I'll listen."

More silence. Roddy struggled with what he was about to say.

"I've had this fire inside me from the time I was eight or nine, fire that at times broke out in full flames burning things down. It was such an angry fire." More silence as Roddy tried to find the words. "But at the camp the fire transformed into a passion for what was right and good. The people, the native people, taught me without my asking to learn, not with words, but more by their actions, their courage, their songs."

"So you do understand."

"But I don't know what it means for me."

"What about the flames burning things down?"

"I burned down buildings," he blurted.

"What do you mean?"

"I burned down two garages and an old depot and nobody found out who did it? The insurance company paid for rebuilding the garages and the city was going to demolish the old depot anyway. I've never told anyone except Gabe, a homeless man who was drunk."

"And you don't know if you can live with yourself. So you told me, hoping that would exonerate you. You're making me an accomplice, you know."

"What do you mean?"

"It means that I now have information about a crime that I should report. If I don't I'm withholding information. That's illegal."

"I didn't think about that."

"No worry, I won't report you. Besides I don't know enough about it and please don't tell me more. Just realize that I can't exonerate you. It's still up to you."

"I thought maybe you'd understand."

"I understand but that doesn't let you off the hook."

"I suppose not." Roddy looked anxious.

"Are you okay?"

"Yeah, I guess."

"So you're guessing again."

"Yeah, I guess." He broke his own tension.

He dropped off Larry Little Bear at his place in Northeast then drove to his home at his dad's place. His mom and Roger were there to greet him. All three worried about his wound but supported him in his adventure. They listened to every word of his story as he related the events of the four days he had spent at Oceti Sakowin Camp and they ate Haraldson apple pie that his mom made with an ice cream topping.

CHAPTER TWENTY-SEVEN

RODDY WENT BACK TO work at the Hardware Store feeling more at home, feeling good about being in his dad's presence, feeling good about his wound that would leave a scar to remind him of a moment of courage and commitment to people that he admired. He felt good about accepting Larry LIttle to Little Bear's invitation to go to Standing Rock, an invitation he surely would have refused only a short time ago. He had taken a stand. He was out there, stepping in, taking part, even though he had no idea what he was doing or why. He stuck his neck out and people responded. He first sensed this change in him by Angela's reaction. She sensed both his confusion and his determination to act, to say, Yes.

He enjoyed the brief talks he had with Martin Scott and Jerry Thomas, both Lakota Sioux with white fathers but dedicated to their native ancestry. What enticed him most was their spiritual alliance with the earth. The earth with its flora and fauna were sacred. They were the incarnation of Wakan Tanka. Now he understood why his camping trips with Marty were in a way spiritual. They were being with the earth. He loved being at Oceti Sakowin. He wanted so much for the people to stop the pipeline. They had to win, but even if they didn't, they had come together as a people.

The Stranger Who Was Himself

On election night his dad, Julia, Emma, Angela, and Jason listened together as the results came in at the Mattson condo to popcorn, soda, and for Jason and Dennis, a Negra Modelo beer. No one was prepared for the outcome. No one even into the early hours of the morning believed that the electoral votes would override Hillary Clinton's popular victory. Only Jason seemed unperturbed. He had indicated in the past month how disgusted he was with Trump's unpresidential behavior, but he still thought of him as an action man that could break up the iron fist of both parties. Both Emma and Angela said Trump's victory meant a setback for women's rights. Dennis said Trump contrived with the Russians to defeat Clinton. Jason kept mum for sometime until he confessed he threw his vote away for Jill Stein. He couldn't vote for either major party. Roddy thought of Marty, of Larry Little Bear, of Eryn Wise and Jasily Charger, and for the earth that this new president had no interest in. The question among them hung in the air. Now what?

Roddy called Marty and commiserated. Clearly Marty was in emotional pain, frightened, confused, disbelieving, anxious about the well-being of his family.

"What has happened to this country that we escaped to and might now have to escape from to somewhere. This country was our hope. This was America, the land of the free. Now what is it?"

Roddy listened. "I don't know. I truly don't know. But I'll stand by you and my mom and dad will, too. I'm sure of that. And Angela. Angela. He hadn't talked to her. He needed to. Now. He needed her to help him with the fears he now felt for the Martinez family and for the land he loved. He didn't know how to deal with the changes taking place inside him. His past didn't matter. What mattered was now and its affect on the future. He had to be involved with the people he loved. That's what mattered. That would give him courage and meaning.

The next week, Wednesday, if he remembered accurately, Roddy got a call from Jason. "Just called to say how much I enjoyed the time with you on election night and especially the stories you had to tell about Standing Rock." He paused. "Oh, incidentally, I have a prosthesis, well I don't have it fitted yet but it's here at the Vet Hospital waiting for me. Just thought you might want to know."

"What do you mean, incidentally. For God's sake man this is huge." They laughed almost to tears with the joy of it. Jason was getting a leg, a new leg. He'd be able to walk soon. "My God man, this is incredible. You've been waiting so long."

"Not so long really. I'm getting along pretty well without it. I'm a little scared. Maybe it won't work right. They say it takes a while to get used to it. Anyway, tomorrow, I go in for a fitting and instructions and begin physical therapy. You want to come?"

"You want me to come? Really?"

Jason nodded.

"I'm honored. This is big. Ya, I'll come."

"Good. Angela and Mom will be there, too, but I'd like you to come."

Roddy wondered why he, a 17 year old kid, had become a close friend of this brave and complicated man. It made him feel necessary once more.

The prosthesis fit. Jason stood tentatively afraid to move, but he did as the therapist demanded. There were adjustments to be made, digital hookups that allowed his brain to be in command. Roddy watched while perspiration beaded on his forehead in a cool room. His hands clenched. His legs tightened as if he were the one who had to learn to walk. God this was scary and thrilling and amazing.

Nearly overcome with emotion, Jason took three steps then clutched the therapist. This was too much, no not too much, he would continue and he did, several more steps. Then he, too, sweated both with the effort and the excitement of realizing this was going to work. He would learn to walk. This leg would become part of him.

Roddy, Emma and Angela exited while the therapist, Bill Hanson, explained to Jason the procedure for removal and attachment and the procedure for adaptation. At least that's what the three thought was going on. The therapist told them that Jason was to be completely independent. He shouldn't need his mother and sister to assist him. Within two weeks he should be walking without a walker or a cane. It depended on him and no question Jason was determined to walk. He would walk. He would train. He would make that leg his accomplice in victory. Together they would win the battle.

What thrilled Roddy even more was that Jason decided he would travel with the vets to Standing Rock in mid-December to serve as unarmed shields in the combat attire to protect the protesters from police and national guard assault. This would be a test of his leg and garner the same metal he needed to survive in Afghanistan. Roddy had inspired him. His new leg was the impetus and the challenge. This was not Roddy's mission. He would watch on TV thrilled to see his hero standing up with other vets against injustice.

Then Jason, on the advice of his therapist, decided he would have to take his stand on crutches rather than on two legs. The severe December cold could impair the digital workings and could get cold enough to cause frostbite of his pelvic area.

Rather than this information being a deterrent, it provided further impetus. After all, he had become adept with crutches and what could be more impressive than a maimed veteran standing in the cold against those that would taint the land. Warily all concerned seconded the motion with prayers and good thoughts. And that prompted Roddy to make a request.

Overcome with resolve Roddy encouraged his mom and dad, Roger, Emma, Angela, Jason, Marty and Juanita to volunteer at the American Indian Center to serve Thanksgiving Dinner donated by several supermarkets. The dinner was open to everyone and everyone came, hundreds, actually, all day long. Roddy thought about Darrell who had served others from off the streets thankful for a meal and a place to sleep. The Center was a community serving people. David Finch was there, all healed up and exercising his skill in accommodating those who needed his help.

"Glad to see you," he said. "You have what it takes."

What did that mean? What did he know about Roddy, really? David's words startled him. What does it take? Who was he in this conundrum of possibilities? What he knew for sure was that his father and mother and closest friends were here because of him and that was good. What he knew was that he wanted to help people.

For the next several days he wrote a journal, at first on a school narrow lined tablet, then in a hard cover blank book, then on his MacBook. He described every moment of his adventure in North Dakota. He gushed about Jason's amazing adventure with a new leg that he called Magic Man. In spite of the outcome of the national election, good things were happening. He had good people surrounding him, his people and so many new people he cared about. But he delved into his past, too, telling the truth about his behavior, reassessing his anger and his behavior toward his parents, but not the fires, not yet. He didn't want them in print. What mattered was that he told himself the truth, the truth as he perceived it. Everything he wrote was not only therapeutic but also visionary. He was searching for his future.

Then in early December in the blistering cold Jason along with nearly 20,000 veterans stood as shields against the oncoming police and national guard. Television news cameras scanned the crowd of people in parkas and combat gear against the fierce-some weather. There bolstered by facilitating veterans stood a man with one leg smiling into the camera as if he were posing for an Emmy. As far as Roddy was concerned he was. As the camera paused on Jason the reporter mentioned the hundreds of veterans gathered in support of all those who demanded the oil company stop its threat to the earth and its people and that included those present in spite of disabilities. "Very impressive," she said. Yes, it was, yes indeed.

CHAPTER TWENTY-EIGHT

AFTER CHRISTMAS CAME the fearful beginning of the transfer of power from Obama to Trump. None of his family or friends wanted to talk about it. The feeling ran deep and confused. No one knew for sure how to think of the future. Jason had completely turned against the anti-gay, racist, misogynist Trump and didn't want any of them to talk about it either.

Then on foggy, windless, mid-thirties January 21, a day after the Trump Inauguration Roddy joined Angela with nearly 100,000 women and men supporters in a St. Paul rally in opposition to Trump's agenda. And in Washington D.C the rally was the largest ever in the capital city, between 500,000 and 1 million, 3 times as many as those who attended the inauguration the day before. But it didn't bother Trump. He simplify lied about the numbers and boasted that women supported him. Roddy knew what side he was on. Now he had to learn how to behave with that awareness.

In the meantime the Standing Rock demonstration dispersed. The camps were sterilized and the pipeline snaked its way toward Indiana per Trump's orders. The anti-Trump crowd was clearly growing, however, and the Women's March had engaged more people than anyone expected. Soon investigations into Trump's financial backing, his appointees, and Russia's involvement in the election would garner his base and incite his opposition. Talk show hosts loved him for easy comic material often with parody that would humiliate anyone with a slight chip in his egotistical armor, but encouraged him to sport more vicious tweets. For most citizens the election was over, the president installed and life moved on—sort of.

Roddy worked full time now for his father in the hardware store, but was restless, undecided what he should do. His past crimes continued to haunt him like a ghost of himself very much alive and parading about in his dreams. He spent time with Angela mostly at the bakery. He wanted to woo her but wasn't comfortable doing so, not because of her response to him, but because of his unworthiness. He believed she cared for him. Their time together had supported that. It was that he wanted to protect her from himself. Maybe he had to reveal himself and end their relationship. Certainly, she would not want to continue it after his confession. Yet he couldn't do that. If she was interested in him instead of the fellow he knew she was dating, then he was wrong for leading her on. Worst of all, his affections may not have been perceived as he thought. Any romantic overture may bring embarrassment. So he didn't woo. He didn't press. They were good friends who enjoyed each other's company. It was complicated.

Except for a few cold days in early February, the month was warm for Minnesota, even reached into the 50s by the last week, enough heat for strolls in the parks. It was Angela who suggested a walk in the Hopkins Park where she and Roddy had watched the sunset the past summer. Roddy couldn't refuse but knew that their relationship was reaching a crucial point, one that demanded honesty. He would have to tell her the truth.

On the same park bench of their earlier sojourn, they sat side by side as the warm sun heated their skin beneath their jackets. They said nothing for a while as they watched the rivers of melting snow swirl toward the street drain. What a lovely day. It would be a shame to spoil it, but spoil it he must.

"Angela, you and I are good friends. We've had many good conversations. You've shared some inspiring poems with me and I've appreciated your confidence that I could absorb them. We've marched together for the same causes."

"I agree." She paused. "Is there something you want to say? You seem to be saying what we already know." She studied him, wondering if she should cut him off.

"I have done some bad things." He paused and waited for a response. She waited anxiously.

"In moments of anger the burning inside has led me to burning things." Roddy continued on with a full confession while Angela sat stunned. When he finished, she was looking at her feet as if she thought they might start walking or maybe dig themselves into the concrete to avoid embarrassment.

"And you are telling me because?" Her eyes confronted him, forcing him to continue.

"Because I've decided to turn myself in." He hadn't intended to say that, but he did, and now he had to do it.

"To the police?"

"Yes." He mulled over the consequences of such action.

"You could go to jail."

"Maybe, but I was fourteen at the times. I was a juvenile. I don't know what the penalty will be. But I have to tell the truth, and the truth is that most of that anger is gone, not all of it, but most of it and what isn't expresses itself differently. What's changed is that I feel needed. My parents have changed, too, since the divorce. They treat me and Julia like we matter. We can talk to them. I don't know how they will react when I tell them my story. As far as I know they haven't a clue about what I've done.

"I know you were angry when you first came here. I didn't want to have anything to do with you at first. But I saw you changing. You listened to the poems I recited. You stayed in school. You and my father hit it off very well. I saw that. You befriended my brother and became his good friend. And then you made signs and demonstrated at Standing Rock. I like how you've changed. And now you've decided to take responsibility for your actions. And I'm honored that you've told me."

"Will you come with me to the police?"

"Yes, but first, I think you should tell your parents. If you want I'll be with you when you do."

Roddy fidgeted as if he could squirm out of the discomfort. He knew she was right.

"Okay, just you and Mom and Dad, Okay?"

"And Julia?"

"Yes, and Julia."

That was Friday evening. On Saturday Carmen brought Julia to the Mattson condo about five. Angela was there as planned and Dennis was in his bedroom reading. Roddy sat them down across from each other with Angela and Julia on each side of him and explained that he had something to talk to them about. Neither looked happy about it, fearing something but not knowing what. They sat in shock as Roddy poured out the series of events that had haunted him for three years. He included the feelings of neglect that made him feel insignificant and unnecessary, but he explained those feelings as if he was standing outside of himself, calmly and without accusation.

Carmen blurted out, "It was your father who. . ."

"Don't start, Mom. This isn't about blaming. You two were not good together and because of it you weren't good for us. I don't blame you. I did, but I don't anymore. And I don't blame Dad. I know that you love Julia and me. You've shown that in many ways since you've been divorced and even before, even though I was too angry to notice. You are both happier. You are not fighting. You pay attention to us."

Both parents sat in silence while searching for words that might matter at the moment but couldn't find them. Roddy continued.

"Will you go to the police with me?"

"What, you're going to the police?" Dennis was aghast. "You can't do that." This information was too sudden for him to think it through. He reacted in a protective mode.

"I have to, Dad."

His dad said nothing, perhaps imagining what this confession would mean.

Julia threw her arms around him and almost whispered, "Now I understand in the hospital when you said you were sorry about the matches."

It was Saturday evening, a busy night in town, a busy night at the precinct station. One officer behind a window inquired what they needed. When Roddy said he wished to confess to the crime of arson, the officer appeared nervous and exclaimed into the microphone, "Have a seat, I'll be with you in a moment."

He put down the mike and pressed an intercom button. Within a minute another uniformed man appeared through a door in the back of the entry room. "Hello, I'm officer Blakey, how may I help you?" He usher them into a back room that might have been used for interrogation and told them he was going to record Roddy's statement and Roddy began his confession.

When he had finished the officer seemed sympathetic, almost complimentary in his response recognizing, apparently, the courage it took for this young man to make his statement and face possible incarceration. He said they would check the records of the arson incidents to be sure that Roddy was a minor when they occurred which would make a considerable difference in the penalty the judge was warranted to issue and likely to give. Then he dismissed them placing Roddy in the custody of Dennis who agreed with Carmen that he should be in charge while they awaited the call to court. So they waited until the middle of the week when they learned that Judge Nelson would hear the case and pronounce sentence.

CHAPTER TWENTY-NINE

LIFE AT THE MATTSON home had not been as tense in many months, but the tension was not between father and son, but from fear of the unknown. What would the judge decide? Would he go to a detention center? Probably not since he was seventeen, almost eighteen. To jail?

Maybe. Would he have to pay back the insurance company for the burned garages? That could take him years. By confessing had he set his own life aflame? Were the past burnings now burning his future?

He had two more weeks to stew over the possibilities. Then on Tuesday, March 7, he stood before Judge Nelson, a middle-aged woman of pleasant demeanor, in juvenile court. All of the people Roddy requested were there in support: Dennis, Carmen and Jack, Emma, Angela, Jason, Larry, and Marty. When Roddy had met with him at Taco Bell, Marty, too, understood the tension under which Roddy had lived. He was determined to support his friend in any way he could. He was there now in court nodding his approval to Roddy as he awaited the judges decision.

The courtroom wasn't as Roddy had imagined. Rather than dark wood paneling and high church like gothic windows, it was a modern room, well lit, with plain glass windows overlooking the bustling street below and a long blond conference table with chairs around it and the judge sitting at the far end. It didn't appear that the sentence about to be delivered would come from a lofty place and indelibly mark him, but rather from a position of compassionate justice. Some of Roddy's anxiety waned in hopeful anticipation.

"Roddy Dennis Mattson," the judge began. "You have confessed to two serious crimes of arson that you committed approximately three years ago. I have studied your case very carefully. I've talked to the victims of your crimes, in one case private citizens, in the other public property, and with some of the people you have brought into this court this morning. Your parents have gone through a difficult divorce that made your life miserable. That does not excuse your behavior. Your sister went through the same kind of trauma and while not unaffected, did not act out the way you did. I have learned, however, that you and your parents have been doing well together, that you, after several truancies and failing grades, have graduated from high school and been employed in your father's business and that you traveled to Standing Rock in protest of the pipeline and were bitten by a police dog. There was no indication that you provoked the attack or that your anger got the best of you. So let me ask you, why did you burn down two garages and a dilapidated depot?

"Your honor, I was angry at the way kids treated me in school. The one garage belonged to the family of the kid who tormented me the most. I wanted to burn down his garage in revenge for beating me up. I know it was wrong. But I didn't believe that for a long time, not until I felt I mattered, that somebody cared about me. Now I know the people in this room care about me and I care about them. And the depot? I was angry because that was my homeless friend's hangout. It upset him when the city boarded it up and he no longer had it as his place of refuge, so I burned it down. Again, my action was wrong. It seems, however, I did them a favor."

"Maybe, but arson is a crime. I appreciate your coming forward and your honesty. You are underage to be prosecuted as an adult or too old for juvenile detention. I've had to think long and hard to do justice to the law and be fair to you. I've made my decision. First, I want you to go through a series of psychological examinations, and second, I sentence you to 150 hours of community service that you will arrange with this court. Also, I've assigned a probation officer to monitor your behavior and report to me monthly. On March 21, the first day of spring, you will present to me the ways by which you will serve out these hours as a volunteer to make some sort of amends for what you have done. Do you understand what I am requiring of you?

"Yes, your honor."

"And when you are angry, do no harm. This court is adjourned." The entourage of supporters leaped from their chairs and showered Roddy with hugs as if he had scored the winning touchdown in the Super Bowl. Roddy caught a glimpse of the judge over his mom's shoulder as she paused by the door and allowed a smile to cross her lips. Tears of appreciation watered his eyes. He had a future and it was for him to decide what it was.

CHAPTER THIRTY

ARNOLD, A FRIEND JASON had met at Standing Rock, gave up his St. Paul apartment and together with Jason rented an apartment in the Uptown of Minneapolis so that Jason could be nearer to his mother's bakery that they operated together. Together the two men developed plans to expand the bakery to included a coffee shop and discussion center where each evening one or the other would lead a conversation on current topics of interest. To entice participants, they invited local authors to exhibit their literary accomplishments and sign books. Visual artists decorated the walls with their latest work. The aromas of baked bread and fresh ground coffee, enhanced with the exhibits soon made it necessary to monitor the verbal input of the numbers of people with a talking stick and inner/outer circle arrangement. While the discussions proceeded Emma and Angela (when available) moved among the guests with bread, wine and cheese. Angela continued to pursue her degree in English education at the University.

While the men recreated the bakery, with Emma's blessing, Emma and next-door-hardware-store owner Dennis were making plans of their own. For example, as Emma's Bakery was becoming a coffee shop and an evening salon, Emma and Dennis, now rarely separated, were developing Mattson's Ace Hardware into a complete bicycle shop and landscaping center. In order for both adventures to be successful the four entrepreneurs bought out the land behind them with financial aid of a joint loan to facilitate the expansion and to create an atmosphere inviting to shoppers all day long. Roddy's contribution besides moving from hardware to landscaping was to entice entertainers, for donations only, to perform on Saturday nights during the summer months. At first, the performances were few, but by mid-July the word was out and performers were as abundant as the crowd. Before long each business hired two more employees to meet the demands. Often they shifted from one business to the other accordingly especially since Roddy had other obligations. Cars and bicycles filled the Paradise Valley Shopping Center to the delight of all the businesses so located.

On March 21, Roddy presented his volunteering plan to meet the requirements of Judge Nelson's sentence and probation officer's oversight. Until he turned 18 in May he would work with David Finch, who provided him with opportunities to dole out food stuffs at a food shelf near the American Indian Center and via the Center to transport people in need to clinics or AA meetings and even to help young people with summer school lessons. These activities helped Roddy feel needed even as he provided for the needs of others. He calculated that if he volunteered for five hours a week, he would satisfy his sentence in 30 weeks or about the first week of November. He could do that easily. And then after his 18th birthday in May he could volunteer with Habitat for Humanity and use his hardware skills to good advantage and to learn more and help people to help themselves erect homes for their families. Roddy had all the data clearly written with contact information of the people he would work with and for.

The judge was impressed, but no one was more impressed than Roddy himself. He had a vision based on what he had discovered really mattered to him. In spite of the political scene, he would become a positive force for what was good and right. He could accept the challenge.

Marty continued at Hamlin University throughout the summer, but was able to squeeze in a bike trip with Roddy from time to time. Most often they headed west to Lake Minnetonka where they would lunch from their back packs and talk. His parents, he knew, were vulnerable to Trump's whim and needed to draw no attention to themselves. Even a traffic ticket could spell doom. In the meantime he, Marty, would do what he could to protect them, whatever that demanded. Hide them if necessary. Maybe flee to California where the citizenry was more amenable to immigrants and the authorities more ready to overlook the executive orders.

Roddy mused about the changes taking place in his life. Jason's successful adaptation to his new leg and his heroic stand at Standing Rock made him smile. And the exciting plans for the expansions of Mattson's Ace Hardware and Emma's Bakery that offered more opportunities for him to explore marketing activities from bike sales and repairs to landscape design and flora acquisition. He could work making lattes at Emmas, repair screens and replace glass in windows, or deliver bagged ash trees or buckeyes in his dad's new (actually used, but new to him) Ford 4x4 pickup truck.

But that was later. For the time being he was still seventeen and had volunteer requirements from court order. That, too, offered opportunities to learn and help. Via David Finch's encouragement and his remembrance of Darrell and Gabe, (What had become of him, prey tell?), he made sandwiches for the homeless at the main Minneapolis food shelf and then helped to distribute them to the four affiliated food shelves throughout the area. In Blue Moon on Mondays he picked up food supplies from supermarkets and churches to fill the shelves. He liked this work. He met people. He found himself smiling and conversing as he had never done before. He wasn't a loner anymore, not much of the time. Still after his daily volunteer activities and his paid job at the hardware store, he often mused and moped. Musing was more productive, but moping was more part of his history and reminded him of his failures. At times he blamed his parents. At times he condemned himself for his past behaviors, then brightened with the realization that he had confessed to his crimes to his parents and the law and he was paying a small price in atonement. So now who was he? Where was he headed?

By his 18th birthday on May 9th, he had completed 35 hours of volunteer service and was now old enough to become part of Habitat for Humanity and the Hennepin County Fix-it volunteer program. He liked nothing better than fixing things, building things, solving mechanical problems and helping people. His hardware store background had spurred his interest as if it were a stallion ready to burst from a race track stanchion. From that time on throughout the summer he chalked up the hours on new construction working side by side with families erecting their new homes or refurbishing older homes in bad need of repaired window sills, concrete foundations or eaves and gutters and a coat of paint. He loved the work and he was good at it. And he loved the paid work as one of the three employees at his father's store. His life was good, loaded with possibilities if he could choose one of them.

CHAPTER THIRTY-ONE

HE HADN'T SEEN LARRY Little Bear for several weeks, Larry who had prodded him into making a stand and discovering a cause worth fighting for. He decided to pay him a visit at his auto shop. It was a beautiful day in June in the mid 70's when he drove up to the garage door and read the sign. CLOSED. Closed? On a bright sunny morning? Why? He peered through the garage windows to discover that much of the equipment was gone. His friend had moved, but where? Roddy had a phone number and tried it several times. No answer. His heart pounded at the thought of losing contact with his friend, of not knowing where he was or whether he was okay. He remembered the circle of demonstrators around the fire at Standing Rock in the chilly autumn air and the Lakota stories and songs. He knew that experience was part of him for ever. Larry Little Bear was a spark that ignited the fire that would burn down part of his old self so that the new Roddy could take root in him.

It was several days later that Larry called him from Standing Rock where he had taken up residence. He explained that his mother, who lived in Northeast Minneapolis, had died and his best friend had moved to Cleveland and business was spotty. Evidently, people assumed a Native American offered cheap service because he wasn't accomplished or trustworthy or was simply a lesser human being. The old ugly prejudices were fomenting again. Why? He could guess. Anyway he decided to take his pickup loaded with as much of his equipment as he could, and with all his skills to help his people back home, to live out his life with them, to help them keep their community together after the failure to stop the pipeline, to support the regeneration of the community he loved, to keep them from despair and alcoholism, to teach them his skills, and to survive on little income. He wanted to not only support the old ways, but also to encourage the young and their parents to get an education and to support the schools. And he encouraged Roddy to go to school, college or trade school, but go to school, to learn. It was clear to both men that they missed each other, and yet in spite of their time together fighting for the same cause, they were from two different worlds and would go their own ways. But Roddy was welcome at Standing Rock anytime and invited to pay a visit. He would. He said he would, but it seemed unlikely even as he said it. So Larry was gone from his life but not from his memory or the lessons he had learned from him. When he happened by that auto shop on his route delivering sandwiches later in the summer, he found it restored, open and operating as a Starbuck's coffee shop. The transition was complete, no sign of the Indian past. It had been stashed away on a reservation someplace, by choice this time, but not really.

Of great interest to Roddy was the developing relationship of his dad and Emma who worked so well together next door but often side by side, often talking, sometimes laughing, sometimes just looking at each other.

"So what about you and Emma?" Roddy inquired slyly at breakfast one Saturday morning.

"I suppose it's obvious that we care about each other."

"I'd say so, yes. Tell me."

"Well, we've talked a lot about our future. We have one, you know."

"Together?"

"Yes, I think so, but we don't know about it yet. Now that Jason has moved out but is really the one in charge of the business and Angela is about through school and involved with a man that she has decided on."

"What?"

"What do you mean, what? You knew she was engaged, didn't you?"

"No, I guess I didn't." Roddy was stunned. "Could we talk about this later?"

"Of course. I'm sorry if I said what I shouldn't. I didn't realize. I'm sorry."

"Let's talk later." Roddy got up from the table and shut the door to his room. On this sunny morning the clouds hung from the ceiling. What was he thinking? Somehow he had thought Angela and he were bound together, that they were soul mates.

They had shared so much. How foolish of him to assume that she thought of him with the same affection that he had for her. What did their time together mean to her? Not what it meant to him, apparently. He was angry. He was on fire, the old fire of rejection, of a nobody, lost. He realized that he had counted on her as a foundation, an emotional support that would get him through all of his angers. He had made his first real confession to her. Was that where it went wrong? Did she see him as unworthy as he saw himself. A confessed criminal? Damn his life. Damn what he had done. Damn her for allowing him to deceive himself. He was a grown, eighteen year old man, sobbing into his pillow. How could he face her? What a fool he was to not see that the two of them were just friends. After all she was almost three years older and in college and he an uneducated boy with a criminal past. Damn it all. He had thought his confession and his atonement was the start of a new life. Now he had to start all over without Angela. First Larry then Angela. Damn.

There was Marty. Of course, there was Marty.

But before he could think that relationship through with all of its complications, the phone rang. Angela. She was calling him. Should he answer? What should he say to her? What was she going to say to him? He hesitated until it was too late. The phone went silent. He had let the moment pass. What could he possibly say to her. He didn't know she was serious about this guy. In fact, she hadn't mentioned his name. Then, boom. She was engaged. When was the last time they talked? Two weeks. Why didn't she tell him then? Damn. He seemed to be saying that word a lot lately. No, they would never be lovers, but they could still be friends. At least he thought he could be friends with the woman he thought was everything. But then he was only eighteen, not old enough to get serious. She was, however, now about to turn twenty-one. Maybe those years difference would seem meaningless in years to come, but right now at this transitional time in both their lives, the years might just as well have been ten or even twenty. Just friends. Could he accept that? He didn't know. He had to call her and pushed her button on his smart phone.

She didn't answer. Why? She had just called him. Maybe she realized she couldn't find the right words. Maybe she knew how he felt about her and didn't want to see him hurt. Maybe, she wasn't thinking about him at all.

He wrung her out of his mind for a moment as if it was a wet sponge. That's what it felt like as he turned his thoughts to Marty in summer school to hasten his years of college and law school. If anyone could cut academic corners it was Marty. Maybe Marty would grow out of Roddy's range, a huge oak tree standing above a weeping willow. Bull shit. They were never equals but that didn't stop them from being friends. It was just that Roddy was smothered in a blanket of doubts right now. He was a young man with infinite possibilities of which none were apparent. He called Marty. No answer.

Roddy remained alone in his room on his bed looking up at the stars in his ceiling as he had so many times before and for the moment wished that Julia was there with him as a comfort. She always comforted him even when he had been cruel to her poking pins in her dolls or tossing lit matches in her direction. God, he was a creep. The two of them hadn't spent much time together lately. She was becoming an excellent dancer, even offered a position in Minnesota School of Dance and gladly accepted. That kept her busy. She had little time for anything else. Good for her. She knew what she wanted and pursued it.

His pillow was wet. What a baby he was. Forget all this shit. Damn it. What he needed was to get out of this lonely room. He stood and gazed at himself in the full-length mirror he had installed to remind him that he needed to present himself to the world. He had a presence if he allowed himself to stand tall and wear a smile. The smile had to come from counting his blessings. It was about time he did.

The phone rang in the kitchen where he had left it. He let it ring then went to it. It was Marty. He left a message "Meet me at Sonny's Cafe in an hour. Let me know."

Roddy texted that he'd be there. It sounded too urgent not to be.

Roddy found Marty at a corner table alone staring out the window. When Roddy approached, his friend rose awkwardly and gave him a hug as if he would never be able to do it again. They had hugged before but always a kind of see ya hug as a reminder that no matter how many days or even weeks passed without an outing they would always be friends. This hug was different and Roddy knew it.

"What's happened?" He asked, afraid for the answer.

"I've had to drop out of Hamlin. My family . . . "He paused to gather the strength to continue. My family is moving to California.

It's what I thought might happen. ICE is approaching, snooping, you might say, and if they come to our door step, Mom and Dad could be sent back to Guatemala. They have to leave. Now. And I'm going with them. I have to. Clarissa and Pedro are going to stay with their baby, sweet little Martina. We'll miss them so much."

Roddy sat dumbstruck then gathered a few words of inquiry. "How will you get there?"

"In the pickup. It's the only transportation we have."

"The three of you in one seat?"

"We'll manage."

"Where will you go and what will you do there?"

We'll go to the San Joaquin Valley where migrants find work. Dad will provide whatever services he can to meet the demands of those people, maybe find a job in Fresno. Who knows? And Mom, I don't know. She might find a child care job. We'll see."

"And what about you?"

"I hope to continue my education at Fresno State College when we can afford it. Until then, I'll get a job and help the family."

Only at that moment did Roddy realize the import of Marty's message. Not only was his friend leaving, no doubt forever, but his brilliant mind was on hold. He may never find a way to become the engineer he so wanted to be. For the second time in a couple of hours tears flooded his eyes. This was too much. This was so unfair. God damn Trump. God damn this country's failures to provide opportunity for its best people and this immigrant family was some of its best people. This time Roddy initiated the hug, one that may be the hug of a life time.

The two young men stood for minutes not wanting to let each other go. Roddy felt the gravity of Marty's family situation. These people didn't deserve what was happening to them. And Marty and Roddy should not have to be jerked apart by a president that had no concerns for anyone but himself.

"When do you leave?"

"Tomorrow, we're packing the pickup today."

"Can I help?"

"Thanks, but this is a family thing with Clarissa and Pedro and Martina. Mom wants these moments with her granddaughter."

"Sure. So I won't see you for a while."

"No, nor I you," trying to lighten the burden of this parting.

"Well, duh." They laughed weakly.

"Do you need some money to get there?" What a foolish, desperate question.

"We've saved enough, but thanks, no. We'll be fine."

Roddy knew that wasn't true, but he understood what Marty meant.

The waiter had observed the scene and knew better than to approach to ask for their order. When he did, the friends demurred. "We've decided we're not hungry, sorry."

"I hope things work out for you," the waiter nodded knowingly, not from what he had heard, but from the body language of the men.

The two smiled and walked to the door.

"See ya."

"See ya." After a moment they turned and walked their separate ways.

Now what?

Roddy felt that his heart had no home. He had let it roam once Angela helped him discover he had one. Maybe he was discovering it himself when his curiosity in searching for Darrell took him outside of himself. He had feelings for him in an inexplicable way. But Darrell died and Gabe was no replacement, only for an episode of a drunken confession. But maybe there was more to Gabe than he allowed, maybe he was more than a homeless drunk. Still he seemed so distant, not a friend, nothing like what he had become with Jason, who was still his friend even though he only saw him at the complex he, Arnold and Emma, Angela and Dennis, yes, Dennis, who was clearly becoming a part of the family. But what would he do without

Marty? Would Marty be all right? Maybe he should follow him to California, work in the fields, learn about migrant workers as he had about the Native Americans at Standing Rock. That was an important awareness for him. It taught him to use the fire inside to create instead of destroy. It gave him hope for a better world and for himself in it. And Angela. Angela. That's a story he didn't want to write, a story of his humiliation, of thinking that his past and his lack of education could somehow disappear or slowly burn away until his tempestuous past would turn to ashes and be swept away in the wind. Angela, who he thought had the same affection for him as he for her and now she was engaged to a guy who Roddy was sure had nothing to offer her except stability. He was sure she didn't love him. How could she. She hardly mentioned him and suddenly he was to be her husband. No way. He felt the fire again, anger, a boiler steaming over the fire, then despair. Who was he to talk about her fiance'. He, who had nothing to offer her except companionship. He loved her poems. He loved talking to her. He loved looking at her. She had been so receptive to his confession, supported him all the way, but deep down she must have been judging him, dismissing him as a friend she had had some fun times with, but now she had to move on. Was that it? He was a has been who never was?

God, what a fool he was, a no good, stupid, uneducated fool.

He had to find Gabe. But what he found was that there was no Gabe. He, too, had left, gone to Florida, Peter said. There was no Gabe. Maybe there never was. Maybe he had imagined it all—the Old Barn, Darrell, the ashcan, the homeless shelter, even the fires. No, the fires were real. He had confessed and paid the penalty. That was behind him. He had to believe that.

He had to find a niche, but where did he fit? Now here he was talking to Peter, a counselor at the homeless shelter, in his office looking down over the cubicles of beds for the night, telling Peter about his brief times with Darrell who froze to death and Gabe with whom he got drunk, and now had gone somewhere warm, and his own adventures with Larry Little Bear, who returned to live in Standing Rock, and Jason, and Marty, and Angela, whom he loves, who is engaged to a pre-med student. He didn't even remember his name. It didn't matter. Peter listened. When Roddy all teary-eyed had stopped, Peter almost whispered, "They haven't left you. They remain in your heart. You have meant a lot to them, you know. You gave of yourself for them. They won't forget you. Gabe went to Florida to join his brother, Earl."

"Earl? Who's Earl?"

"I know you've met him. They were always hanging out together until they had a major fight over Gabe's drinking. Gabe called him Shithead. And Earl called Gabe Fartface. Terms of endearment, I guess. They were very close ever since their parents were killed in a car accident when they were eight and ten, and the boys were put in a foster home that turned out to be abusive from which they ran away. They got into trouble, joined a street gang that actually befriended them, gave them a family apparently until the leaders got shot up pretty badly and the boys ran again, this time to the streets and a homeless encampment.

"Gabe told me he was a teacher who fell in love with a student and that she loved him back and then he was forced to resign."

"I don't know why he would make up that story, but it isn't true. He has no education."

"Why would he tell me that?."

"Maybe because he wanted to be loved and to blame others for not allowing it to happen. I learned his real story from him after he and Earl ran from the gang.

There were three then, Gabe, Earl, and Darrell. Gabe told me all about it before he took off. Then after Darrell died, it was the two of them again. They had always survived together and they will again."

What a story. Roddy sat dumbfounded, trying to make some sense out of the moments he had spent with them separately. But the others were always nearby observing the relationship of Roddy with Darrell, fascinated by this kid, no doubt, who seemed to have everything, but thought he had nothing.

And Gabe at the memorial for the homeless, nodding to Roddy when Darrell's name was called to indicate that he was Roddy's friend and thereby maintaining a connection with the young man, a connection that led to a drunken night, just the two of them, after Earl, or Shithead, had left for Florida. And Roddy's confession, that if nothing else, allowed Roddy to hear his own words of admission and maybe that admission was the catalyst that brought him to the real thing.

The Stranger Who Was Himself

He was glad he came to the shelter, sad that Gabe was gone, but relieved to find Peter to talk to, Peter who evidently had paid attention whenever he showed up, Peter who knew all about these homeless people and worked hard to help them get back on their feet and now was willing to listen to this confused young man who was struggling to find himself in the midst of prosperity, in the confusion of anger, loneliness, and blessing.

"May I call your dad or mother?" Peter asked.

"My dad, thank you."

Shortly, his father was there thanking Peter, a well groomed man in his fifties with goatee and mustache, mid height and welcoming smile.

"He wants to go home," Peter slipped in, "but I don't think he knows where his home is. He'll need you to help him find it in himself."

Dennis returned a smile, a puzzled smile, not sure what his role should be, but aware that he had one he hadn't tried before.

The two, Roddy and Dennis, rode home together without a word, but aware of a bond between them. Dennis was not about to scold. He was listening to the silence, hearing the need between them. And Roddy was listening, too, and hearing his father's need to be here beside him. Something was happening that neither had experienced before. Things were different now. They both knew it.

CHAPTER THIRTY-TWO

THE NEXT MORNING AFTER a night of restless sleep Roddy pulled the door open to the hardware store and there was Angela. He couldn't face her. He walked to the back of the store without acknowledging her presence. She followed him, determined to force him to hear her. She trapped him behind the work bench.

"Listen to me. Will you listen, please?"

"What can you possibly have to say?"

"How about I'm not engaged."

"What?"

"I'm not engaged, Roddy."

"But my father said. . ."

"I know. I told Mom that Michael asked me to marry him and she got all teary eyed and hugged me and ran off to tell your dad who took it to mean I had accepted. I hadn't. I didn't. Yes, Michael is a good man, a great catch, but not for me, not now. I'm not ready to get married. When he proposed I felt such anxiety, It seemed marriage was what he wanted rather than what we wanted or I wanted. I wasn't ready and besides . . ." She paused waiting for the words.

"Besides?" Roddy waited unable to breathe.

"Besides." She paused stumbling for words. "Besides, I want to continue with school, get a master's degree and become a teacher. I want to teach kids about words."

Roddy said nothing, pondering what her decision meant for him, almost smiling inside and not daring to inquire. At least, she wasn't going to marry what's-his-name. Maybe she cared about him, Roddy. But she wasn't sure and wasn't ready for any commitment.

Certainly, Roddy wasn't ready for her. Not yet. She was amazing and he wasn't, not yet. He wanted to be amazing for her.

This was the third time in a few hours he was all teary-eyed, this time for joy.

Then he blurted out, "When Dad told me you were engaged, I was lonelier than I've ever been in my life."

"I don't want you to be lonely." She smiled as she looked him in the eye, then said, "I found another poem for you. Let's go to the bakery coffee shop and I'll read it to you."

Once seated she began:

Love After Love

The time will come
when, with elation
you will greet yourself arriving
at your own door, in your own mirror
and each will smile at the other's welcome,

and say, sit here. Eat.
You will love again the stranger who was your self.

Give wine. Give bread. Give back your heart
to itself, to the stranger who has loved you

all your life, whom you ignored
for another, who knows you by heart.
Take down the love letters from the bookshelf,

the photographs, the desperate notes,
peel your own image from the mirror.
Sit. Feast on your life.

It's by Derek Walcott. It's what I want for you.

"That's what I want for me, too.. ". He dared not say more.

    Roddy's depression had left him. The fire had ebbed to a warm glow that encouraged him to do what he had to do. He and his dad had talked. He knew he supported him in what ever he wanted to do, even offered to pay for his training whatever he decided that was. And Angela cared for him. He knew that now. They were friends that may in time lead to more.
    Roddy finished his required volunteerism by the middle of November, just after he started his first semester of college at Normandale Community College taking courses in art, sociology and journalism per the encouragement of David Finch, who, if you remember, was treated for dog bites in Mandan and who had suggested volunteer opportunities that would challenge his skills and compassion. He wanted to be more than a volunteer. He would start by going to school and see where it would lead him. He knew, too, that he loved the hardware store with its

bike shop and landscaping center, and the bakery and weekly entertainment that he had started. His future was a mystery, yes, but an exciting mystery. No matter what path he chose, he would stand and walk for those less fortunate than himself and that sooner or later he would be able to look in the mirror and learn to love the stranger who was himself.

The End

www.ingramcontent.com/pod-product-compliance
Lightning Source LLC
LaVergne TN
LVHW011936070526
838202LV00054B/4677